I0521412

The Saga of Lyn:
Book Two
The Quickening

Aric Carter

Copyright © 2018 Aric Carter

All rights reserved.

ISBN:
ISBN-13: 978-1-941469-03-3

DEDICATION

This book is dedicated to those who feel lost and alone. We are only alone as we wish to be, and home is carried in your heart.

.

ACKNOWLEDGMENTS

I would like to thank my mother, Lonna Carter. Again without her help and support this book would not have been possible.
I would also like to thank everyone who enjoyed book one and encouraged me to continue writing.
And a special thank you to Marlo Garnsworthy for helping make this book the best it could be.

CHAPTER I

"Yes, please tell me what it is that frightens you most."

-Hael Atos

Hot magma belched and roiled in the caldera of Mount Hael. It was the highest peak on the westernmost point of the singular continent that was Krysin. Heat from the continuous flow of lava kept the steep slopes clear of snow. The caldera itself remained high above the clouds that ringed the waist of the immense volcano. Streams of fire flowed down from the heights to create blackened fields of desolation for miles surrounding the solitary peak.

Above the lake of boiling magma floated an obsidian citadel. The structure virtually encompassed the entire caldera, making an artificial cap on the mount. The base of the imposing stronghold glowed from the heat below. Without the heat from the caldera, the gargantuan fortress would have been a giant block of black ice. The magical power of the cyne placed around the citadel allowed those who dwelt within to breathe in the thin atmosphere. Without the shield, death was certain.

On the planet Krysin, anyone who could focus their thoughts into a singular image with exquisite detail could bring that thought into reality. This magical ability was called cyning and those that could cyne were called cynosures.

Hael Atos sat on a throne made from the various bones of creatures he had spawned using his power to cyne. Bones of rock reavers, sixton bears, vilekin, grimble, six-striders, booglun heads, and even the head of a dragon formed a grotesque seat from which he ruminated. The massive chair rested upon a raised dais of tiered obsidian. Women of great beauty lounged about the steps on pillows and various animal skins. Food and wine filled the nearby low tables.

Atos' reign was supreme. No one could challenge his rule. Somehow, he knew what those around him were thinking, and if their thoughts were subversive, the punishment was severe and public. Many feared their thoughts would betray them, and this fear kept everyone in check.

The handsome figure that sat upon the skeletal throne looked no more than middle-aged. Long slender fingers rested upon his chiseled cheek. His thick white mane of hair fell about his delicate features to rest upon his shoulders. With each shallow breath, his muscular frame rippled with power. Hael's inky pupils floated in his otherwise solid white eyes.

He waited.

He had been waiting for some time now. After a few thousand years of absolute rule, Emperor Atos had done everything his heart desired. However, he knew what was coming. So, he had bided his time until now. The game was about to begin. Atos so loved to play games.

Hael had felt the disturbance from the east. Cynes had been placed throughout the towering mountains of the Hittons to warn him of any intruders. He knew something alien had taken hold deep within the near impassable range. Ever since the earth-shattering quake months ago, Krysin had not been the same. Because of this new presence, his creations were being pushed out from the mountains. Atos had directed his Dread Knights to the Hitton foothills in preparation for the coming assaults.

For several weeks, wave after wave of his created terrors had been subdued. Then metallic-like spiders had poured forth from the towering peaks. At first, his Dread Knights were decimated by the creatures' terrible beams of fire. Hael had never seen creatures that possessed such a powerful weapon. After he directed his legions to change their armor to reflect the fiery beams, the attrition had nearly ceased.

Hael had watched each battle through the eyes of his Dread Commanders. With the simple use of cyning, if he so chose, he could possess the body of anyone within his realm. He rarely used the cyne anymore, but lately in battles it had come in handy. The carnage had been exhilarating to watch.

Another cyne placed on the distant mountains far to the east alerted him that an interloper had entered the near impassible Hittons. Ages had passed, and Hael had waited for this day to come. He knew the man upon the six-strider would arrive soon. With the coming of the stranger, an age would end. A new era would begin. Preparations needed to be made, and then the sport could begin in earnest.

With a single thought, Hael summoned his Dread Lord to his audience chamber. The empty space before the raised obsidian dais filled in an instant with the presence of a colossus sheathed in an otherworldly set of full plate armor. Standing fully eight-feet tall, the Dread Lord gazed through red-glowing slits directly into Hael's eyes.

Yes, Milord, communicated the titan with his thoughts. His cyne armor was so devoid of color that even the suns' light was not reflected by it. Only the thin rectangular slits in his angular helm displayed any color. The suit was seamless and smooth throughout its surface. The Dread Lord's two-handed battle-axe handle jutted out from behind his left shoulder. Topped with two wickedly curved blades, the head of the vicious-looking axe extended from behind his right hip.

Hael actually spoke aloud. His soft, melodic voice filled the grand chamber. "I have a task for you. A man comes from the east. He is dressed as a Dread Commander, except he carries an extremely unique sword. Punish this false commander; bring this sword to me." Hael finished with a thought, showing him an image of an armored man riding a six-strider in the vast range of the Hittons.

It will be done, avowed the goliath. With that, he turned and marched from the chamber.

Hael leaned back and waved for a goblet of wine. *Let's see how this interloper fares without his beloved sword*, he thought.

*   *   *

Light from the suns did not last but a few hours in the deep confines of the towering Hitton peaks. Tegain had to slow Vyckie to a walk in the boulder-strewn fields between the bellies of the mountains. He had followed the gouges in the rock left from the metallic spiders as best he could, but it had become all but impossible to find their trail. Snow and fog had obscured any tracks. The feeling of impending threat was his only guide now. They had continued from the climactic battle at Talenshan relentlessly day and night for the past week, and still there had been no sign of the metal beasts or any other creature. Tegain's cyne-enhanced armor gave him an ever-present sense of danger from the southwest that grew stronger with every passing day.

Vyckie's smooth, slick coat had quickly become long and furry. Traversing the rough terrain with her six legs, the powerful unflagging charger had covered an extraordinary distance in the days following the battle at Talenshan. Her breath was expelled in a frosty cloud from her muzzle which was covered in shards of ice. Snow, boulders, and steep inclines did not seem to faze the sable steed.

Storms in the Hittons were violent and carried unyielding raw power. Gusts of blinding snow barred his vision of anything beyond a few feet. They were just cresting a saddle between two jagged peaks when a distinct sensation intruded upon Tegain. A new threat had manifested in his immediate vicinity. Scanning the horizon in all directions, the only variance he noted in the whiteness was Vyckie's black mane.

But something was out there watching, waiting. He could feel it.

Tegain leaned back on his haunches and halted the big mare. She stomped at a frosty snowdrift with her forefoot. Vyckie tucked her head at the poll and rounded her neck to block some of the biting flurry from her face. She nickered a deep-throated complaint against the weather.

"What could be out in this?" asked Tegain.

You are. But, I understand your concern. Whatever it is, it probably isn't going to be friendly, said Lyn.

"Indeed. Perhaps we should seek some shelter until this passes. I don't want to run into something unfriendly without being able to see." A feeling of foreboding washed over him. Not wanting to risk being out in the open, he turned her away from the new sensation and back the way they had just come. Continuing in blizzard conditions, they dropped lower into the canyons between the mountains. However, as they slowly traversed the steep, snowy slopes, the fresh feeling of immediate danger dogged them.

As they dipped into the shelter of the peaks, the punishing snow-laden blast lessened to a degree. The whine and hum caused by the slicing wind in his helmet eased as well. Tegain had not realized how loud the howling of the tempest had been. He reached out to stroke Vyckie on her shoulder. The powerful mare was a wonder, and Tegain was grateful to have her as a companion. He hoped the conditions were not too extreme for her. She thrust up her head and huffed as if to say she was all right.

Without warning, the whiteout began to intensify. Even Vyckie's sable mane faded from view in the gale. She halted, unsure where to place her next step. Tucking her muzzle to her chest, the mare tried to defend herself against the stinging wind.

"Hmm, what now?" said Tegain.

May I suggest using me to make a shelter out of the side of the mountain? said Lyn.

The sweeping feminine curves of Tegain's sword twinkled in the fading light. Lyn had long ago imbued her soul to the cold hard steel blade to save her people. Through the magic of cyning, she was able to communicate to whomever wielded her. Lost through the centuries, she had turned her back on humanity until at last she had met Tegain. The loss of his family and his kind heart had drawn her to help Krysin once again.

He received an image of him using Lyn to melt away the snow and cut into the rock face to create a cave. Tegain dismounted and sank to his hips in the loosely-packed snow. Grasping Lyn by the hilt, he unlimbered her as he clambered up the slope a little way. Setting his feet apart in a wide stance, Tegain easily drove the sweeping form of the blade into the side of the mountain.

Lyn flared with intense heat and jets of flame. Snow burst into steam and billowed out all around him. He worked the blade back and forth, and the steam subsided as he cleared away the snow in front of him. He began to see the solid granite turning to molten rock and flowing out down the slope. In a relatively short time, Tegain had made a cavity large enough for Vyckie and himself.

As he waited for the rock to cool, drifts of snow built up to block the entrance. Tegain kept the snow at bay until he could no longer see the orange glow. He called to Vyckie with his mind. The powerful mare plowed through the deep snow to stand next to him. They hunkered down in the back of the newly-erected sanctuary and waited for the storm to pass. Within moments, the entrance was blocked by blowing snow. Vyckie gave a low nicker as the light in the refuge faded. Before Tegain could even ask, Lyn blossomed to illuminate the tiny space.

"Thank you," he said.

My pleasure, said Lyn.

The blizzard continued to rage. It growled and wailed beyond the barrier of snow. Vyckie calmed and lowered her head. The six-strider took in an expanded breath and seemed to relax as she exhaled. Tegain did the same. The menacing presence that had pursued them appeared to have lost them in the squall and was now fading off to the north.

Lying down to stretch out his legs, Tegain relaxed for a time. His thoughts drifted with the sounds of the storm.

He could hardly imagine all that had transpired over such a short time. Only a few months ago he had been a simple innkeeper. Surrounded by friends and family, his life had been blessed and happy. Then the stranger had arrived.

In an instant, with a single beam of fiery light, the stranger blasted his inn and everyone he knew into oblivion. He had barely escaped from the burning inn with his life. The loss of his wife, Shae, and daughter, Gwyn had been almost too much. He had wanted to die. However, the criminals Neil and Gerral had interrupted his mourning. If he had only known what they would do, he would not have let them go.

The day after he lay stunned before his destroyed inn, the Hooded Lantern. Neil and Gerral arrived not to help but to loot whatever was left from the destruction. Tegain chased them away after they tried to rob what they thought was his corpse. He would meet them again in the ruins of Tiris.

Vyckie found him in the Harkon Wood after he escaped from the village of Folsum. Having angered the head of the thieves' guild in Talenshan, she had been hiding out in the haunted wood. She had fallen in love with Tegain. Hoping to gain some answers, they had set off together to the Crystal Trine, the home of the Masters.

They had travelled as far as the Minar Plains when the Masters had met Tegain at the top of a plateau. The Masters told him to find answers in the distant mountains called the Hittons. They asked Lyn to prepare Tegain for the dangers that lay ahead.

Lyn remembered a powerful magical armor from long ago. The soul armor had been trapped beneath a toppled statue in the ruins of Tiris. While trying to recover the ancient armor he now wore, Neil and Gerral had attacked from the shadows. Vyckie had saved his life by taking a spear meant for him.

Tears welled up and rolled down his cheeks. He missed them. He missed the two burly helpers, Hes and Jon. But the loss of Shae, Gwyn, and the rogue girl Vyckie was more intense. Tegain had loved them, and they had loved him in return. They had been innocent. Why did the ones he loved most have to be taken from him? What had he done to deserve this? Tegain spiraled down in regret and self-pity. A warmth settled over him, and he knew it was Lyn.

All is not lost, she soothed.

"I know. I miss them, though."

I believe they are closer than you know. I do not think your naming of this magnificent steed a coincidence. When she arrived, you knew without question that somehow Vyckie had returned. I believe there is a balance to the universe. Nothing is lost; only its form is altered. Perhaps their passing has caused a change that was necessary. How could we know how all of this fits together? It is impossible to conceive of things beyond our knowledge. We must trust that all is as it should be.

Tegain considered what Lyn had shared. It did feel right in a way. However, it did not lessen the feeling of loss. Knowing that Vyckie might still be with him, but now in the form of a six-legged mare called a six-strider, was somewhat of a comfort. His heart ached. A soft nudge from the raven-hued mare's muzzle nuzzled Tegain's head. She stomped a hoof on the cave floor to make her point.

"How do you know what I'm thinking?" asked Tegain.

Vyckie gave a low nicker and nodded.

I think she is connected to you through the armor somehow.

"She is a mystery, but I am glad to have her." Tegain paused a moment to consider. "I do feel it is Vyckie."

The sable mare pounded the rock with an anvil-sized hoof. Sparks and bits of stone sprayed from the forceful blow.

I think you have your answer.

"It just seems so impossible."

Vyckie shook her head and nickered her disagreement. The magically enhanced sight provided by his soul-infused armor seemed to be bright. He felt compelled to take off his helm and see the mare with his own eyes. She placed her soft muzzle against his head and gently rubbed his cheek. The lick from her warm, wet tongue rocked his head to the side. Tegain laughed. Fresh tears flowed down his face. Without a doubt, he knew it was she. The how of it he did not know. Feeling overwhelmed, he stood and hugged the powerful mare around her neck. She curled her neck to hug Tegain as best as she could. His spirit was buoyed from the knowledge that she was still with him. Her warm soft pelt soaked up his tears of joy.

"How did I not notice until now?" he wondered.

We only see that which we choose to see.

"I've been so focused on getting to what attacked us at Talenshan that it had not even crossed my mind. I think I was trying to avoid the pain of her loss," said Tegain.

It is understandable.

"I am humbled, and I am grateful." A peace settled over him, and he reclined against the back of the chamber. After a time, sleep overtook him. Even Vyckie lowered her head and seemed to relax as Lyn dimmed her light to let them rest. Outside their shelter, the bitter tempest roiled and raged.

*   *   *

Kharaxsis wheeled higher to rise above the clouds and driving snow. Still, many of the highest peaks of the Hittons towered above him. The permanently snow-capped mountaintops pierced the grey gloom to be bathed in the bright light of Solis and Solar. Some of the highest peaks were unreachable, even for him. The towering mountains nearly touched the blackness of space.

The drake beat his bat-like wings to gain altitude in the thin air. From wing tip to wing tip, they spanned over three hundred feet. Brimming with spikes and horns, the drake's angular head embodied fierceness. Unblinking obsidian orbs absorbed the surrounding serenity. A long, thin, inky neck connected his head to his broad bulk. His midnight-scaled body was thick with muscle. Kharaxsis' clawed forelegs were slightly smaller than his powerful hind legs. His long snake-like tail whipped behind him, its tip ending in a sharp, horned spike. From his snout to the tip of his tail, he stretched nearly the span of his wings. Perched on his back was the dark, impassive Dread Lord, barely visible against the scales.

The ferocity of the snowstorm had prevented them from navigating any closer to the false dread commander. It would pass. The dark-plated figure was unperturbed. To him, the passage of time was of little consequence. He would wait out the storm. And when it was time, he would complete the Master's task. The Dread Lord was as devoid of emotion as his armor was of light. His sole purpose was to carry out Hael's command. In the past two thousand years, he had never failed.

CHAPTER 2

"It be unfortunate that sometimes a kind word be gettin' ye further than ability."

-Karl Dunmire

It had been weeks since Karl had seen Tegain fade into the Hittons. Now he wished he had gone with him. Master Bennett and his council had declared him the City Marshal for saving Talenshan from the horde of hideous creatures of the vilekin swarm. The vilekin had descended from the Hittons. Half rat and half spider they had truly earned their name. Thousands had survived the siege, and they credited it to the heroics of Karl and his men. He had tried to decline, but even the guards from Folsum agreed he should lead the defense of the city.

Karl had thought his time as a soldier was over. He had retired to pursue his dream of being a simple trader. Making a great deal on goods made him feel better than winning any battle. It appeared that life would have to be put on hold again. Karl had conceded to their pleas and taken the office, albeit without the ceremony.

"No need to put on no show for me," he declared when they had brought up the idea. When they persisted, Karl added, "Be glad I be taking the post." That had ended any further overtures.

Sent along the Trader Way to Crossroads, a rider relayed the news of what had transpired in Talenshan. He was to inform Captain Marshal Donaldson at the conclave and ask for assistance. The Royal Waymen Dragoon's Conclave was the focal point of the city of Crossroads. Rising out of the city center, its fortifications towered over the surrounding squalor.

Keeping the peace and defending those in need were the very reasons King Tulane's Waymen Dragoons had come into being. However, over two thousand years of politics and power-mongering had degraded the once honorable corps into a bloated bureaucratic behemoth. Their ranks had dwindled since Karl's previous tenure. Peace had been the norm. Since his time, most outlaws and bandit kings had been put down.

Having received the news from the messenger, folks from Folsum began arriving just two days later. They were seeking safety behind the walls of the city and the hero of Talenshan. Even Captain Brent and the rest of the guards arrived with most of the townspeople from Folsum.

"We convinced the Folsum city council that until these monstrosities stop coming out of the Hittons, we would be safer with you inside these walls," relayed the stalwart captain when he had arrived.

"'Tis amazing ye be convincing councilman Markus of anything to be doing with me," begrudged Karl.

"Oh, he was the only one who didn't agree. He is still back in Folsum." Brent looked back over his shoulder. "I give him a day at most before he shows up," allowed the perceptive captain as he turned back to face Karl. They shared a laugh.

Even with the influx of people from Folsum, Talenshan's population was still a shadow of what it once had been. The city of over one hundred thousand had been decimated to less than a few thousand. Many of the homes and streets remained abandoned. Of course, all the upscale domiciles had already been reclaimed. Fights had broken out at first until Karl had instituted a lottery system for all the desirable homes.

Cleanup in the city from the vilekin siege had been fairly straightforward. No human corpses remained within the metropolis, and the only severely damaged structure was the city hall, which had been burned by Karl and the Waymen. Only the stone walls of the edifice remained standing. The roof had been totally consumed by the blaze, leaving what they thought was a hollow shell. However, upon closer inspection, the dark bowels of the building revealed something strange. The walls, floors and ceilings had burned away, exposing a hardened black substance that had survived the fire. It had turned the interior into how a termite mound might look if made from obsidian. The wrecked entrance of the city hall seemed to be the only way into the warren.

After some debate from the city council as to what to do about the structure, Karl had simply asked for volunteers to help him with the task. And so, he, Franc, and Thom had ventured into the darkened catacombs to ensure that the entire vilekin host was slain. Light from the trio's lanterns had revealed a grisly truth. Within the black walls, bits of human bone and pieces of clothing could be seen sticking out in places. They concluded that to create their abominable abode, the vilekin must have used some sort of excretion containing the consumed bodies of the Talenshan inhabitants.

Clearing the vile warren had taken the better part of a day. The pitch-black passageways hid a multitude of putrid horrors. Bug-men seemed to materialize from every direction. Often the fiends used their spider-like mobility to drop down from the cavernous ceiling. The queen's chamber had been the most revolting. It had been packed with eggs and larva in various stages of growth.

They had continued until the catacomb was cleansed of every trace of living vilekin. With the task completed, the exhausted trio had collapsed on the grand steps of the transformed hall.

"I think I be happy if I be living the rest of me days never seeing these beasties again," said Karl from the top steps as he warmed himself in the late afternoon suns' rays. He began his ritual post-combat cleaning of his gear.

"Aye, I couldn't agree with you more," said Franc. He lounged just below Karl with his two long swords to either side of him.

Thom grunted and nodded. He sat cross-legged at the top of the steps. His sword and long dagger lay crossed on his lap. Looking to the setting suns, he squinted in the brightness as he spoke. "I don't think we've seen the last of these and whatever else is coming out of the Hittons."

"Aye, ye be right, Thom," said Karl. "'Tis only the beginning I be thinking. The metal beasties be causing all of this, I be certain. I have a feeling that be where Tegain be heading in the Hittons."

"Hard to believe he was the innkeeper," said Franc.

"Did you see what he did to those things? It was like lightning from the heavens was coming out of the sword!" said Thom.

"And he seemed not to be hurt by those lights they were using," said Franc.

"Aye, I be thinking I be parting with a certain sword for far too little," said Karl. "'Tis being in the right hands, though."

"You sold him the sword?" asked Franc.

"Aye, I be selling him the blade," said Karl. "It be looking like a rusty plow when I traded a farmer for it."

"What about the armor?" asked Thom.

"I don't know where he be getting the armor. I suspect he be visting the masters at the Crystal Trine."

"I wonder if they gave him the armor and taught him to cyne?" said Franc.

"Ha, ye be not learning to cyne like he be cyning in such a wee time. But that armor and steed be coming straight out o' legend. I be seeing those in a tapestry in Rytin many a year ago. The Dread Knights be nearly wiping out all of Tulane. If it not be for a certain sword..." Karl shook his head and grinned as he came to the sudden realization.

"What is it?" asked Franc.

"I be seeing that sword before. It be centuries. But I be certain," said Karl.

"How old are you, Karl?" asked Thom.

Karl looked up and to the left as he thought. "I forget, but I be now remembering seeing that there blade held by King Tulane."

"King Tulane!" exclaimed the two swordsmen in unison.

"You mean *the* King Tulane who united all the lands?" asked Franc.

"Aye."

"*The* King Tulane, the one whose name is given to all the lands east of the Hittons?" demanded Thom.

"Aye, he be the one," said Karl.

"But that would mean..." said Franc. He seemed to be contemplating the massive expanse of time, then simply asked, "How?"

"I be not knowin' the how of it. As long as I've been a Wayman, I be always looking the same," said Karl.

"Cynosures used to live long lives. Perhaps you can cyne," said Thom.

Karl dismissed the comment with a wave of his hand. "Nah, I be no cynosure. I be a Wayman. I be making no cynes."

In truth, Karl was acutely aware he had some kind of cyning ability, but he maintained that he was not a cynosure. His advanced age had been the by-product of his military discipline and his strong desire to be the best wayman he could be. Every time the suggestion arose, he would immediately dismiss it.

Karl had never wanted to cyne. As a young boy, he had always wanted to be a wayman dragoon. Riding horse into combat and defending those in need had been his boyhood dream. The fact that cyning had made it possible for him to spend nearly two thousand years doing the very thing he loved did not ease his mind. He had always been a little afraid of cynosures and what they could do. And after the Following's Cleansing, Karl had an even greater aversion to the idea of being able to cyne.

He had not been a part of the Following or their crusade to cleanse the lands of cyning. Karl had not believed the cynosures or the Masters to be malevolent in any way. Nevertheless, he had seen fear and ignorance persuade many to perform unthinkable acts. The leader of the Following, Kaerin Kabe, also had an uncanny ability to incite those around him into a frenzy. Those caught in his thrall were wild in their devotion. Karl had seen many innocent bystanders and defenders of the cynosures fall to his crazed zealots. He did not care to recall those dark days.

"I be thinking this here hall be perfect to defend from attack. It only has one entrance, and it be rock hard. I be intending to be using it as a keep," Karl suggested to direct the conversation away from himself. Franc and Thom shared a dubious look.

"Really, that place is creepy," said Thom with a look back at the charred building.

"And dark," said Franc.

"Bah, if ye be knocking out some windows, it be all bright and cheery," said Karl as he lay back and rested his head on his hands. Both men shook their heads and chuckled to themselves. They lounged on the steps until Solis and Solar had settled just above the eastern rooftops of Talenshan.

"I best be getting back to the barracks," said Karl from his repose on the steps. "The council be wanting to know the status of our undertaking for sure." He rose and gathered his belongings. "Be seeing ye soon."

"Aye," replied the two swordsmen.

Karl left the two men and headed for the barracks in the south of the city square. Coordinating the city guard was almost a full-time endeavor. With the help of Captain Brent, Karl was able to keep the walls and city streets patrolled with a meager number of trained men. Training of the new men was going apace. Many of the newly arrived folk had wanted to join ranks with the hero of Talenshan. Even Jeorg and his band of rogues asked to be a part of Karl's growing militia. He had taken the newfound fame in stride, using it to acquire the things he needed to defend the city properly.

At first, the Talenshan council had been very agreeable to most anything Karl suggested. Such was their gratitude for what he and his men had accomplished. However, he could see that he was wearing out their patience with each new encounter. Karl had never been much for politics or political systems. He was a man of action. Councilmen and their ilk had never seemed to accomplish much in the way of good in Karl's mind. Only on very few occasions had he seen a man of true character—a man possessed with the mind of a warrior who could wield words like a weapon on the field of battle. These rare men had inspired those around them to accomplish great things. Alas, the few councils he had seen were bereft of one of these unique individuals. Karl knew he wouldn't be winning over anyone with any kind of eloquent speech. As he had done for centuries, he let his actions speak for him.

Karl had begun running the city like a military camp. Every able-bodied person was set to a task of either preparing defenses, making arms and armor, training, or support. Supply depots had been set up in strategic points around the city. From those protected areas, food and supplies were distributed to the citizens. He had even stationed supplies in the sewers in case another withdrawal was necessary. The newly cleansed city hall would act as a perfect central fortress.

No one had escaped the appointment of a duty. Even the council members had been seen building blockades and serving food in one of the many supply kitchens. Some of the folk were not happy being forced into service and had voiced their complaints to the council. So far, with the help of Harold Bennett, Karl had made the council see the need for the drastic measures. If the metallic beasts returned, he wanted to have a fighting chance.

Immediately after Tegain's battle at the gates of Talenshan, Karl's tasked Jeri to collect what was left of the wrecked metal beasts. He wanted to know how they could create such a powerful force from their small metallic tubes. After a week of study, they had been unsuccessful at getting the salvaged weapons to work. Fortunately, Ben Kord, a clockmaker, had survived the siege of Talenshan. Karl had enlisted his skills to help with the reverse engineering of the metallic parts. He was confident that, with enough time, they would discern what made them work.

The second most important task had been collecting and creating as many mirrored objects as possible to deflect the deadly beams of the metallic army. Karl suspected that any mirrored surface would be able to reflect the metal spiders' light weapons. He had watched as his friend was assailed by uncounted numbers of the beams. Tegain had looked to be struggling mightily against the assault, until suddenly, his dark armor changed to reflect the searing lights. The red rays had then been deflected to burn holes in seemingly everything around him. With their weapons no longer affecting Tegain, the beasts stopped using them and tried to overtake him. Karl had never seen such a display of raw power in his entire life. In a matter of minutes, Tegain had wiped out an army of thousands.

Karl was now certain that Tegain's sword was the very one King Tulane had carried with him. Stories of the amazing feats accomplished by the king and his blade had seemed to Karl to be heavily embellished. However, now he thought that perhaps they were a little tame in their description. As he recalled, the sword had been lost when the king had died suddenly during a trip to Brac in the south. Karl hoped his friend and the blade would be able to stop whatever was attacking from deep within the Hittons.

"Marshal Dunmire!" called a familiar voice from behind. Karl turned to see Master Bennett walking at a brisk pace to reach him.

"Aye, how be I of service?" acknowledged Karl.

Harold Bennett had once been a trader of fine wares and, in secret, the master of the thieves' guild in Talenshan, but now with the decimation of the city populace and the need to defend his home, Master Bennett had used his cunning and guile to become the de facto mayor of the ravaged city. He actually took the station very seriously, and he seemed to be very skilled at bending the ear of many of the councilmen. Thankfully, Bennett had sided with Karl and had used his influence to help him prepare the city.

"We have received word from Crossroads and the Conclave there. Captain Marshal Donaldson himself is coming with a full regiment of Dragoons," relayed Bennett as he drew closer. "A bird arrived with the news just a few hours ago."

"Be that so?" asked Karl, the corners of his mouth turning down.

"Is this not great news?" demanded Bennett as he registered Karl's look.

"'Tis good a regiment be coming; not so good the marshal be coming." He stopped to face Harold. "I be not hearing any good word to be describing the marshal."

"But he is the captain marshal, like you were," said Bennett.

"No, he be nothing like me," Karl said flatly as he resumed his march to the barracks.

Bennett had to jog to catch up to him. His frown was deeper as he asked, "What do you mean?"

"Ye be seeing when he gets here. I assume it's not going to be pretty."

"He can't be as bad as you say," said Bennett.

Karl huffed aloud and shook his head. "I be hoping I be wrong, but I be knowing different."

Karl could hear Bennett take in a deep breath through his nose and blow it out forcefully through his lips as he seemed to digest what Karl had just said. Somehow, his permanent look of displeasure seemed to deepen further. Bennett stopped for a moment. Karl strode onward. Karl was sure the rogue's warped sense of honor had put him in his current situation. Bennett probably wanted everything to continue on as they always had before. Now he was realizing those days would never return.

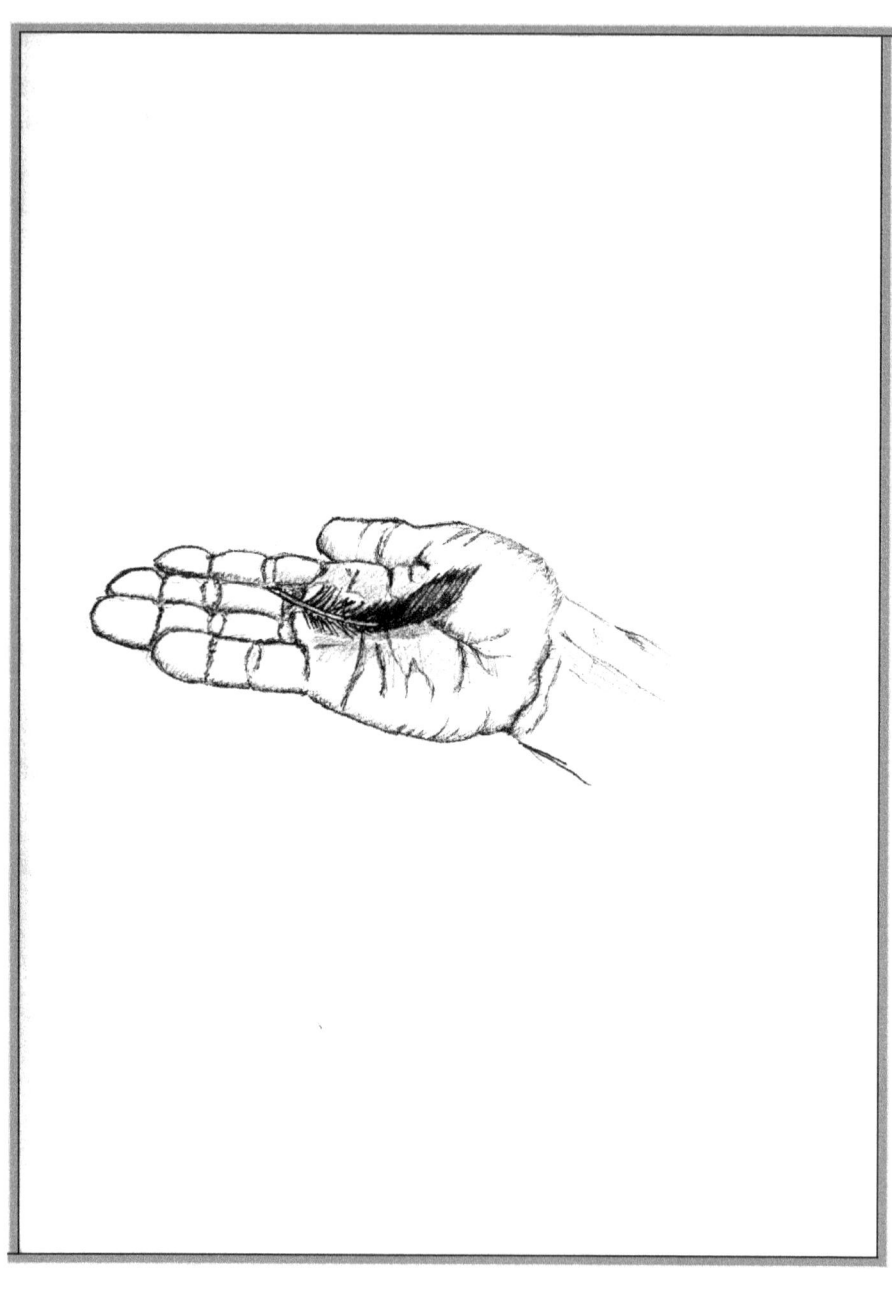

CHAPTER 3

"Solitude, I could not have known myself without it."

-Tegain Hostler

Tegain did not know how long he slept in the impromptu shelter lit by the soft glow from Lyn. However, when he awoke he could still hear the storm raging beyond the blocked entrance. As he began to stir, Lyn bloomed into a soothing white light to illuminate the tiny space. Vyckie nickered softly and pawed the ground as Tegain rose to his feet and stretched.

Good morning, greeted Lyn.

Tegain yawned. "Good morning! If it is truly morning, I cannot tell with this infernal storm."

True, it may not be morning, but you have just awakened. So, it is your morning, no matter what time it may be in the world outside.

"Indeed. You are right. From the sound of it, I believe we are still stuck here."

It would certainly appear so. I have a feeling this storm may last for several days or maybe weeks.

"Weeks?!"

Storms in the Hittons are notorious for their strength and tenacity. Some have reported seeing storms hover about the peaks continuously for months. It is part of the reason they haven't been traversed by any sane person.

"Are you saying I'm insane?" Tegain chuckled.

A tickling sensation travelled down his spine as Lyn spoke in his mind. *Goodness no; however, I think with your armor and steed you can probably do the insanely impossible.*

"You forgot to include the most important piece... you, Lyn. I wouldn't be anywhere without you."

Yes, I guess we couldn't have made it this far without each other.

"Indeed! Let us do the insanely impossible together." He felt the tingle of Lyn's laughter along his spine. "But first we need to escape our self-imposed prison. Do you have any ideas?"

If you could only cyne away the storm, we could be on our way.

"How long does it take to learn how to cyne?"

That is a difficult question to answer; everyone is different. It took me many months to be able to create even some very basic things. Others have practiced for years and never learned. Cyning is more a state of mind and being than anything else. I think it takes so long because no one else can see what is taking place in your mind to help guide you to the proper state. This is where you will have a distinct advantage. I can see what you are thinking and help you achieve the correct state to manifest what you are concentrating on.

"Well, it looks as though I'm not going anywhere anytime soon. How about we start with some cyning lessons?"

Actually, you have already started cyning lessons. Since we left the Harkon Wood, you've been practicing emptying your mind. The clearing of the mind is always the first thing you must be able to do. Once the mind is clear, you can begin to visualize what it is you want to create. At first, it might be easier with your eyes closed, but eventually, you must be able to do it with your eyes open. It is very important that you visualize correctly and perfectly. Many have injured or killed themselves and their teachers trying to manifest the simplest of things.

"Yes, I remember when you had me clear my mind to set fire to the bramble briar in the Harkon. I can see how it could go wrong if one doesn't visualize properly."

Oh, you have no idea. But I am sure you will do fine.

"Hmm, I hope you are right." He wondered if he was making the right decision.

With your armor and me being made of metal, I don't think we have to worry about getting hurt.

Tegain glanced over at Vyckie. "What about her?"

The six-strider took in a deep breath and let it out in a huff.

I don't think we will actually get to cyning anything very soon. But if we do get to that point, we will make certain she is safe.

"Okay then, so what do I need to do?"

First, have a seat—whatever position is most comfortable for you.

Tegain sat with his legs crossed. He laid Lyn carefully across his knees and rested his arms on top of her.

Very good. Now, breathe in slowly through your nose and let the breath out softly through your mouth. Concentrate on your breathing. Feel yourself relax with each exhalation.

Tegain did as he was instructed. He felt his limbs become heavier and his body begin to relax with each measured expiration. Concentrating on taking slow deliberate breaths gradually lulled him into a semi-conscious state. Thoughts drifted in and out of focus.

Very good, encouraged Lyn softly. Her voice seemed to float to him from a great distance. *Now I want you to hold your breath at the end of each intake and exhalation. As you hold your breath, pause your thoughts and just feel your body. If a thought arises, release it with the continuation of your breathing. Try to expand the length of time that no thought arises.*

Following these additional instructions, Tegain held his breath at the top and bottom of each slow respiration. At first, he couldn't pause for more than a second or two. Thoughts would spring up immediately. Images of recent events and worries of what was to come assailed him ceaselessly. His frustration began to affect the exercise. His breathing quickened, and he expelled and sucked in with more force with each passing minute.

Be at ease, Tegain. Your frustration is only causing more thoughts.

Tegain huffed out his held breath. "It's as if I have no control over what my mind is doing. I can't stop anything."

I know it seems that way at first. You have only just begun. Give it some time, and do not become angry with yourself. This is something that cannot be forced. You must allow it to happen.

Tegain closed his eyes, breathed in deeply, and exhaled slowly to regain his focus.

"Okay, I will try and not let it bother me."

Have you noticed your thoughts are of all but what is right here, right now?

"No, I never realized it. How can I keep from doing that?"

Try directing your attention to a part of your body. Let's choose your hand. Continue the same breathing but put your awareness there in your hand. Now, hold your attention and awareness there. Feel it. Become your hand and nothing else.

Tegain focused on his right hand as he continued to breathe deeply. He could feel it there at the end of his wrist. It was warm and pulsed in time with the beat of his heart. Each finger curled inward slightly in a relaxed position. As he concentrated more intently on the sensations in his hand, he registered his body relaxing further.

Then something odd happened. Tegain felt as if his head came forward and down into his lap. Suddenly, he was seeing himself from below as if he were his hand. The experience was so jolting that he immediately jerked his awareness back to his head.

"What just happened?" he asked.

That was very strange. I believe you actually moved your awareness to your hand!

"Is that what is supposed to happen?"

No, that normally takes a very long time to learn. In fact, it is what I do to communicate with you.

"Hmm, was that cyning?"

Yes and no. Yes, only those who can cyne can do it, but no, it isn't a cyne.

Tegain sighed heavily. "Well, at least it is something. I would have to say it was one of the strangest things I have ever experienced."

I also noticed that your thoughts ceased while that occurred.

"Great, how long was I without thought?"

Oh, maybe a second or two.

Tegain had to laugh. "One second." He shook his head. "I have a long way to go."

It won't be as long as you think. You have already done something that takes months or perhaps years to learn. Take heart, my love.

You are right. Thank you, my love, Tegain thought back.

After acquiring the ancient armor from the dread commander, Tegain had found that he didn't require food or water. He also didn't seem to tire very often either. Without the need for much sleep or any other distractions, they kept up their mental practice as the storm continued unabated outside. It was hard to predict the passage of time. Tegain thought that perhaps a day or two had passed, but there was no way of telling, especially with the space illuminated by Lyn's soft glow.

While Tegain and Lyn trained, Vyckie seemed to have gone into some sort of hibernation. The sable steed barely moved. If she did, it was only to shift her weight to a different set of feet. Her eyes were closed, and she didn't appear to be breathing. Tegain still wondered how the black mare had sustained her seemingly unflagging pace without the need for food or water. And now she appeared to suspend herself. He couldn't fathom what other surprises the mythical horse might possess.

It took another three days of constant concentration before Tegain could finally hold a clear mind for more than just a few seconds. Thoughts and worries slowly faded as his mind learned to be still. Once he achieved this milestone, it was if a barrier had been lifted. A deeper calm than he had ever known settled over him. Soon he was no longer struggling to hold his breath between respirations.

Most excellent, Tegain, Lyn congratulated him after he completed an entire breath without a single thought.

"I believe I may be able to hold a clear mind now. At least for a little bit."

Indeed, you can. You've done very well. And in such a short time.

"Okay, so what's next?"

Now it is time to cyne. I want you to create a feather. First, imagine the feather down to the smallest detail. Try to leave nothing out. Know how big it is. Feel the weight of it as if it were in your hand. Make the image of the feather as real as you can possibly make it. Once the image is complete, release it. Then recall it exactly as you created it."

"All right, I'll try. What if I can't imagine it very well?"

Then you might create something you were not intending. Don't worry, I won't let you continue until you're ready.

Hesitantly, Tegain commenced constructing an image of a feather in his mind. It had been some time since he had seen a feather. Recreating one in his mind seemed a daunting task. He started with the quill and then began painstakingly adding the barbs. Several times he lost his concentration, and his thoughts wandered off on some tangent. When he realized the slip, he would pause a moment, take a relaxing breath, clear his mind, and begin again. After what felt like hours, Tegain had constructed the perfect likeness of a single feather in his thoughts.

As Lyn had instructed, he released the vision and then tried to recall it. The image returned almost immediately with a little effort. He did this a few more times until he felt comfortable that he could do it reliably without much effort.

"How's that?"

Excellent, I couldn't have done better myself. I am very proud of you.

"Thank you, Lyn. I can see why most folks never learn to cyne. If not for this forced solitude, I don't think I would have ever had the patience to do this."

Yes, you've stuffed about a year's worth of practice into these past few days. I believe your suit has allowed you to achieve such a marvelous feat.

"Indeed, I think you are right. Come to think of it, I haven't even had to go… you know to the woods…"

A tickling sensation ran down his spine as Lyn spoke in his mind. *Yes, I know.*

"Well, enough of that. Do you think I am ready for the next step?"

Do you think you are ready?

"I don't know what's coming. So, I can't honestly say that I am or not."

Fair enough—you are ready then. Now, this time I want you to keep your eyes open and maintain the state of thoughtlessness. When you are there, I want you to bring forth the image of the feather. Just as you have practiced, don't allow any stray thoughts to arise. Place the image out in the real world. See it there. Know it is there. Finally, you must love it.

"Love it?"

Yes, love it. Cyning takes emotion. The greater the emotion, the stronger the cyne will become.

Tegain was quite dubious.

Think of it as putting oil on a fire; as you add more oil, the larger the fire becomes.

"Love a feather… hmm, all right. I never heard mention of using love to cyne."

The emotion used to empower the cyne will give it strength in reality. The more powerful the emotion, the greater the result when cyning. I personally cannot think of a stronger emotion than love. This part of cyning is never discussed. If one were to cyne with hate and anger, the results could be quite disturbing. With such emotions, natural things are contorted into twisted results. I believe this is how Hael Atos created so many monstrous beings when I was not this hunk of metal.

Tegain took a moment to consider before he spoke. "I see. Well, I think I am ready to give it a go then."

Yes, I know you are.

Tegain took a deep breath and let it out slowly. Keeping his eyes open this time, he let his practiced mind slip easily into the stillness of no-thought. From the emptiness, he brought forth the image of the feather. He held it in the space in front of him. As much as he wanted to love the feather, it was proving to be a challenge. Loving something had always just happened. Tegain had never willfully chosen to love anything. Either he did, or he didn't. The thought that you could choose to love something had never crossed his mind. Emotions were something that just happened. He lost the image of the feather as he struggled to add his feelings to the form.

"How do you choose to love something?" he asked out of frustration.

It may seem that way, but you have always had a choice. There have been times when you have chosen not to love.

"When was that?"

When you were knocked unconscious. As I tried to wake you and made my way through your subconscious, I saw some things in your past. You did not always love your father.

"Yes, but I was just angry."

Who made you angry?

"He… No, I chose to be angry at him," said Tegain with sudden realization. "I have always been responsible for how I have been feeling."

Yes, it is one of the hardest things to realize and one of the most freeing. No one but you controls your feelings. It took me many, many years to come to that realization.

"But you were able to cyne before you were a sword."

Yes, when I was young and innocent, it was easy for me to love everything. But my experience as a sword has caused me to question everything I had ever known.

"I had no idea. I am sorry, Lyn."

There is no need to be sorry. All is as it should be. We are here and now, Tegain. There is no other place I would want to be. Try thinking of something you do love and then try to hold that feeling when you begin the visualization.

"Aye, I think that might work." Looking down at the sword in his lap, Tegain noticed the glinting blue gem set in the middle of the crosspiece. He loved Lyn. The feeling in his chest was unmistakable. Tegain held on to that feeling as he began again.

After several relaxing breaths, he was without thought. This time, as he brought forth the image of the feather in the stillness of his mind, the thought of the blue gem flashed briefly as he tried to keep the feeling of love. And for an instant, the color of the feather changed to blue. He felt a gentle tug in his chest and heard a small popping sound.

A single, perfectly formed blue feather appeared in front of him. Tegain watched as it slowly drifted down and rested on the blue gem of the crosspiece.

CHAPTER 4

"I be gettin' too old fer this."

-Karl Dunmire

They arrived two weeks after the messenger had been sent. An entire brigade of Royal Waymen Dragoons marched into Talenshan as if they had just saved the day. Luckily, Talenshan had remained unmolested since the attack from the metallic spiders. Karl, Master Bennett, and the rest of the council stood on the top step of the city hall as the procession arrived. When the file of riders had finished trotting in, there were over three thousand horsemen in the city center. The spacious square still had room to spare. The commanders and officers wore their full parade regalia. Their armor gleamed in the morning suns' light. Red and gold banners fluttered in the light breeze from the east. It was quite a sight to see.

However, Karl wasn't too impressed.

"Looking to be all for show to me." He looked over to Jeri, Thom, and Franc, who were standing a little lower on the steps. The three men all shared looks of apprehension at the new arrivals. "I be hoping they be bringing their own food."

When the brigade had finally finished making its rank and file formation, a bugle sounded out three sharp notes. Banners were set to parade rest, and the company commanders, along with Captain Marshal Donaldson, dismounted to make their way up the steps to meet with the council of Talenshan.

The captain marshal was not a very tall man. He stomped up the steps with his back held rigid, his flowing red cape cascading behind him. As he drew closer, Karl could see his piggish eyes darting between the men at the top of the steps. The troop of accompanying commanders kept in step just behind their stunted leader. The captain marshal appeared to be judging each man in quick succession. His cursory assessment complete, he veered slightly left to stop before Master Bennett.

"Hail, Captain Marshal Donaldson," greeted Bennett, raising his arms to encompass the gathered army. Your messenger notified us of your imminent arrival. We are honored you came yourself and brought so many of your men."

"You must be Harold Bennett," said the captain marshal, his voice like a metal rake dragged across stones. Karl saw Harold visibly cringe.

"Aye, Captain Marshal, I am," stated Bennett without missing a beat.

"The city of Talenshan hardly looks as if it has been ravaged by untold beasts," declared the captain marshal. "Your messenger would have us believe the town was nearly wiped out. I have only seen one building destroyed, and you stand before it. Please tell me I have not come all this way for naught."

"I assure you, you have not come for naught, Captain Marshal," said Bennett. "Indeed, the Talenshan you see before you has been decimated by beasts from ages past and some new metal terrors from the Hittons. Only one in a thousand remains alive to tell the tale. Talenshan is but an empty husk before you. If not for the brave actions of Karl Dunmire and his men, we would still be trapped in the city sewers."

"Yes... about this Marshal Dunmire," squawked the diminutive captain marshal. "I have never heard of this man. I am the captain marshal of the eastern lands. And to my knowledge, there has never been a Karl Dunmire in service to the Dragoons. It is a crime punishable by death to impersonate an officer of the Royal Waymen Dragoons. I intend to prosecute this impostor as soon as possible."

"Be that so?" Karl interrupted before Master Bennett could respond. Bennett looked askance at Karl.

The captain marshal shot a piercing glance at Karl before he addressed him directly, "Would you be this Karl Dunmire who has been lauded by the messenger and now Master Bennett?"

"Aye, I be he," said Karl.

The captain marshal raised his arm and pointed to Karl as he commanded, "Take this man into custody until we can contend with his crimes against the king." His face had become more and more beet-red, and spittle flew from his lips with each word he spoke.

"Well, that didn't go very well," said Jeri as he drew his sword. Franc,

Thom, and the rest of Karl's men unlimbered their swords to block the advancing dragoon commanders.

"Be holding up there, Waymen," said Karl as he raised his hands to calm everyone. "I be solving this here issue with a few words."

"How so, impostor?" asked Captain Marshal Donaldson.

"It be simple. Ye be not looking far enough back in the rolls to find me."

"Is that so? How far back do we need to go?" asked the irate captain marshal.

"I be reckoning ye only looked back a few decades. Ye best be looking back a few centuries."

"If that is the case, then we will hold you until we can send a man back to verify that what you say is true. But it would be my guess you are impersonating a long dead captain marshal," he surmised.

"I be who I be. Ye yerself be seeing me items all over your quarters in the conclave, Marshal Donaldson."

"Of what do you speak?" demanded the captain marshal.

"Ye be staring at me shield every night ye be putting your eyes to sleep. It be showing a black swallow on a field of gold. Me armor be standing next to your mirror. It be having a small dent just below the left breast. I be sure it bothers ye to no end." His eyes locked with the captain marshal's; he could see the recognition in the man's eyes as he spoke.

"How do you know these things?" the reeling captain marshal asked.

"I be putting them there. Just like the captain marshals before me. It be tradition that keep them there. So, I be knowing that they be still there."

"I would vouch that this man is who he says he is," added Master Bennett.

"Aye," came a chorus of similar replies from all the men surrounding Karl.

"It would seem we are at an impasse," conceded Captain Marshal

Donaldson.

"If ye be looking to the inside of the armor, ye be seeing me initials on the chest plate. I also be registered on the rolls, but it be in the books in Rytin," Karl said as an afterthought.

Captain Marshal Donaldson seemed to swallow the bitter pill of truth with a great deal of distaste. "It may be as you say. I still will be sending a man to verify that what you say is true. Until his return, you may remain as you have claimed to be." With that, he waved his men to return to his side. Karl's men sheathed their blades, and the uneasy air over the group at the top of the steps lifted slightly.

Donaldson broke the silence "Now, as to the defense of the city, what measures have you taken against further attacks?"

All eyes turned again to Karl. As Donaldson followed their looks, Karl barely suppressed the small grin on his face. "I be making the city ready," he declared.

"Yes, Marshal Dunmire was voted unanimously to be the city marshal," affirmed Bennett.

"Is that so?" said Donaldson.

"Aye," replied Karl.

"I will see if the proper preparations have been made," said Donaldson, as he eyed Karl before turning away to address Bennett and the city council.

"Due to the dire circumstances that have befallen Talenshan, I, Captain Marshal Donaldson, hereby pronounce marshal rule. By the power vested in me by King Nycholas, my men and I will require the full participation of the citizens of Talenshan. Anyone found not to be in full cooperation with my directives will be dealt with in the appropriate manner. Now, as to my quarters and those of my men, we will require accommodations befitting our station."

Bennett and the council members looked like cornered rats during the captain marshal's proclamation. Worried glances passed between the council members. This was a totally unexpected turn of events. However, Karl knew enough about Captain Marshal Donaldson to know that the man would be eager to flex his political power. Karl was more than ready with an answer.

"Ye be standing in front of yer new quarters, Marshal. This here structure be the most defensible in all Talenshan. I be hoping to be using it meself, but with ye here, I be relinquishing it to ye," said Karl as everyone looked to him. At first, he kept his goateed face slack in an effort to show no hint of humor or satisfaction. Then he flashed a small frown of displeasure as if finally relenting to the captain marshal.

Seeing the expression that came over Donaldson's face, Thom and Franc had to look away from each other to keep from bursting into laughter. Before he continued, Karl gave them a quick discerning glance. "It be not looking it to the untrained, but I know yer keen sense and military knowledge be seeing the tactical advantage o' this here fortress."

Donaldson's eyes were nearly popping out of his skull as he looked upon what appeared to be the ruined husk of a building. He barely choked out a response through his gritted teeth. "Certainly, I can. However, I will have to further evaluate the tactical advantage this structure can provide for me and my men."

"Aye, I know ye be finding it to yer liking," countered Karl, crossing his arms across his chest.

"Well, now *that* is settled, is there anything else you require, Captain Marshal?" asked Master Bennett.

With crimson features and bulging eyes, Donaldson's head appeared ready to explode. The two nearest commanders edged ever so slightly away from their seething leader. Karl had seen enough. Through the years, he had dealt with many men like the captain marshal. He couldn't help having a little fun. But he didn't want to tempt fate. If Donaldson didn't get his way soon, he would make life very difficult for them all.

"I be certain the captain marshal will be wanting to inspect what's been done to protect the city and be issuing what's needing to be changed," interrupted Karl. He then turned to Jeri. "Jeri, if ye be seeing the marshal's men in to their new quarters," he said, indicating the catacomb of the city hall with a tilt of his head, "I be escorting him and his commanders. Follow me, please." Karl strode between Bennett and Donaldson to break the building tension. He gave a quick wink to Harold as he passed by. Without looking back, Karl headed down the steps and out into the square.

Still boiling with pent-up rage, Donaldson was left with little choice but to follow. Before turning to catch up with Karl, Donaldson snarled as he took in the men standing on the top of the steps.

Karl kept up his rapid pace as he made his way out of the square toward one of the many staging areas. He could hear the booted steps of Captain Marshal Donaldson quicken to keep pace. Karl glanced back to see Donaldson's stiff short legs pumping furiously to keep up. For every stride of Karl's, Donaldson had to take two. Karl purposefully took a circuitous route from the city center. He hoped to exercise out some of the captain marshal's built-up rage. As they stopped at the first defensive position, Karl could see the captain marshal and his retinue were trying desperately not to show that they were breathing hard.

"Here be a staging area for supplies and patrols." Karl spoke loudly enough to be heard over their labored breathing. He had stopped before a two-story edifice that resembled many of the buildings throughout the block. A few small windows and a simple set of stairs to the doorway broke up the smooth stone façade.

"By the Nine, there is no way you are as old as you say you are," huffed Donaldson between breaths.

"I be not lugging around a full set of dress armor," said Karl.

"Be that as it may, I rarely find myself out of breath during a *walk*; it must be the altitude," said the captain marshal. He swept past Karl into the building to begin his inspection. Two guards were sitting in the main room as the troupe entered. They leapt to attention as the captain marshal and his commanders entered. Donaldson waved a dismissive hand at them and asked Karl to lead them on a tour of the facility.

Neatly stacked in various rooms throughout the building were all types of arms and armor, as well as crossbow bolts and arrows. The basement had been converted into a larder that held a multitude of dried goods.

Karl could tell Donaldson was trying hard to find fault with the layout of the equipment and supplies within the building. After completing an intense half hour audit, Donaldson ordered the quarrels of bolts and arrows along with the crossbows and long bows be placed on the upper levels instead of on the ground floor. This seemed to satisfy him greatly. As they continued to each fortified area in the city, Donaldson took great effort to find within each location something wrong that required immediate attention.

Next, they visited the guards' barracks where Captain Brent began a cursory tour of the facility. Instead, the captain marshal performed a thorough inspection of the entire barracks. During the review, he grilled Brent on the current watch schedule for the city. Afterward, he reeled off what needed to be changed in the barracks and the watch schedules. Karl could only shrug and wince to an exasperated Brent before heading out to their next stop.

After visiting the site where Tegain had fought the metallic spider-like creatures, Karl led them to a small warehouse. Here the mangled remains of the metal spiders lay all about in various states of dissection. Behind a pile of metal pieces and parts, a simple-looking man was meticulously studying one of the metal bodies placed on the only table. Candles, lamps, and lanterns of every type provided intense light about the workspace. He looked up from his examination. At first glance, he was an unassuming fellow. His dark, stringy hair flopped down in tangles around his head and shoulders. Looking a little confused, he brushed back some loose strands behind his ears and shielded his eyes from the light as he took in Karl and the new visitors.

"May I help you, Karl?" asked the perplexed man.

"Ben, this be Captain Marshal Donaldson and his commanders. They be inspecting what yer finding with these metal beasties," explained Karl. "Gentlemen, this be Ben Kard. He be a clockmaker. And these be the hordes that attacked Talenshan after the vilekin." He swept his arm out to encompass the completely filled warehouse.

"Ben Kord," clarified the clockmaker. "Pleased, to meet you, Captain Marshal."

Donaldson leaned over one of the many piles to get a clearer look at the things. He absently kicked at the metal heap. "They don't seem to be much of anything," he commented.

"Ye be not seeing them when they be whole," said Karl. "They be cutting holes through anything and from farther than any arrow be travelling. If not for Tegain, Talenshan would be wiped out for sure."

"Hmph," grunted Donaldson. The corners of his mouth turned down. "Where is this fellow Tegain?"

"He be taking the fight to where these beasties be coming from," answered Karl.

"I see. And how was he, a single man, able to destroy this host?" Donaldson waved his hand about to indicate the piles of metal.

"It be hard to explain, but he be having a special suit of armor and a very unique blade," said Karl.

"I highly doubt that armor and a sword did all this," declared Donaldson. His brow furrowed further in concentration. "All of this smacks of a cynosure."

"Aye, it be looking like it. But it be a powerful ancient weapon made from cyning," said Karl.

"I've never heard of such a thing," Donaldson said as he looked about. "Enough of this. Well, clockmaker, what is your assessment of these things?"

Ben brightened at the chance to divulge what he had learned of the metal constructs. "Yes, where to begin? First of all, they aren't really metal," he said as he tapped the creature on his worktable with a metal pointer. The material echoed with an odd hollow sound. "They are some sort of fiber that is stronger than any metal I know. Secondly, they appear to be powered by this box here," he said, indicating the part by tapping on it with the metal rod, "which I call the heart. I have yet to determine exactly how it does it, but the heart emits a type of invisible fire through these wires." Ben pointed to some exposed wires hanging out of a torn arm. "Whatever is flowing through the wires is quite painful to touch." Ben looked to each of the gathered men. "I have found this out the hard way." No one seemed to take note of his warning. He pulled back his sleeves to expose various red marks. "Anyway, the wires appear similar to what carries blood through our own bodies. Like us, this energy seems to be what animates the creature. If the heart is destroyed, the creature is dead."

"Interesting," said Donaldson. "What have you learned of the weapons these things possess? Have you been able to make them work?"

"That has been my main focus," admitted Ben. "Marshal Karl indicated that these tubes here," he tapped the appendage that ended in a cylinder, "are what caused all the destruction. I believe the energy in the creature is concentrated in the tube. Using ruby-hued lenses, the energy is then focused into a beam that has incredible heat. However, as of yet, I have not found a way to get the weapon to emit a beam."

"I see," said Donaldson. "Well, I think I have seen enough for today.

Master Dunmire, if you please, show us to our quarters."

"Aye, Captain," said Karl. "Thank ye, Master Kard for yer time."

"It's Kord," said Ben.

"Aye, I be saying—Kard," confirmed Karl.

Ben lowered and shook his head in frustration as Karl and the company of men left the building.

CHAPTER 5

"There are no words to express the feeling from creating your first cyne. The only way is to do it yourself."

-Tegain Hostler

What Tegain had just done took a moment to sink in. Yes, the feather might be blue, but it was a feather that had not existed until he created it.

Congratulations, Tegain. You have cyned. Very well done!

"I can hardly believe it," said Tegain. Caught by his breath, the feather floated up and away from the jeweled crosspiece. He gently cupped his hand to catch the drifting feather in his palm. "It is exactly how I imagined it to be. Well, except for it being blue."

Oh my, I thought you had made it blue for me," she said with a tingle of laughter. *Nevertheless, for your first cyne, it was beautifully done. I remember my first attempt to make a feather produced just a little white blob. I don't think it much resembled a feather at all. It took me quite some time to give it all the details to make it look right.*

"Thank you, Lyn. I think I'm still dazed by the whole experience."

Indeed, you have accomplished so much in so short a time.

Tegain studied the little blue feather in his hand. He wanted to keep it with him. After a moment, an idea came to him; slowly, he brought the feather up to his breastplate and concentrated on having the armor hold it there. When he pulled his hand away, it was empty. Instead of the old insignia of rank on his left breast, in its place was now a tiny blue feather.

Very nice. I like it!

"It will always remind me of you," said Tegain as he softly stroked the secured feather. In the peace of the moment, he noticed that it was actually quiet. The seemingly ceaseless storm had finally stopped. *Can it be?* he thought.

It would appear so. How fortuitous. It is always good to stop on a high point while training. Let's see if this siege has indeed ended.

Tegain received an image of him holding Lyn horizontally out in front of him and aimed at the snow-blocked opening of the shelter.

"Like this?" he said, lifting the sword into place.

Yes, perfect. Brace yourself. This may knock the snow off the whole side of the mountain.

Tegain planted his feet firmly. He placed a comforting hand on Vyckie's neck. Raw energy bloomed along the length of the glaive. The power intensified for a moment then erupted from the tip in a blast of light and superheated air. Snow exploded into steam from the intense heat, and the force of the burst sent the blockage hurtling far out and down the slope of the mountain. Light from the midday suns flooded the space. For several seconds, nothing happened; Tegain let out his held breath.

"Well, that wasn't so…" he said, as a low rumble began to build from somewhere up the peak. Growing with each passing second, the rumbling soon became a roar that shook the entire mountain. Vyckie stirred from her suspended state to give a snort of displeasure. Tegain pressed himself against the back wall as the thundering crush of snow barreled down the peak and once again covered the opening. The avalanche seemed to be never-ending, but finally, the torrent ceased, and a hush settled over the mountain.

There, I think that should do it, declared Lyn in the intervening silence. *We won't have to worry about an avalanche now. Well, at least not on this peak.*

"I had no idea that something like that could happen."

Avalanches are quite frequent in the Hittons, especially after long storms.

"How did you come to know so much about the Hittons?"

Lyn took a moment to answer. *I think it would be easier to show you.*

Images and sounds began to fill his mind. Soon, the small cave disappeared and only the vision from Lyn filled his mind. Through the eyes of a stranger, a scene began to coalesce. Howling wind wailed, preventing even hearing the man's footfalls in the deep snow. Wind-whipped snow limited vision to just a few feet. Between gusts, he could barely make out the outline of a man in front. A coarse rope appeared to be tethering them together.

The images blurred and re-focused again on a group of heavily furred men huddled together in a small snow cave illuminated by a very familiar blade. Worried faces looked to the man holding the sword. Again, the scene changed, this time showing the men emerging from their snowy shelter. White-topped peaks pierced the bright blue sky. Tegain got the feeling the small party had made it deep into the Hittons.

Before setting out, they tied off to each other as before. Slowly, the group made their way up and out of the bowl where they had made their shelter. The vision skipped again to show the single file of tethered men. Tegain watched from the eyes of the man at the back of the line.

While the expedition traversed the steep snowy slope, the now familiar sound of an avalanche echoed from high above. As the man peered around his surroundings, he stopped as he looked up the slope. The vision locked on a wall of billowing snow speeding down the mountain toward him and his men. Men screamed and shouted. The man held up Lyn and pointed her at the coming onslaught. But nothing seemed to happen. He cursed the blade as he cut himself free of the line and drove the sword into the side of the cliff before the blast of snow overtook him.

Tegain's vision returned to normal as Lyn spoke. *Derrick Hitton carried me through most of his adventures before he died of a fever while exploring the swamps that cover Brac in the south of Tulane.*

"I should have known," scoffed Tegain. "How else could the greatest explorer ever known survive all those fantastic adventures?"

Indeed, how could he? What you saw was his attempt to cross these peaks, which were eventually named after him. He was a restless soul. Always wanting to see what was beyond the next rise, and more was never enough. His curiosity drove him and those around him into many perilous situations. Of course, the entire expedition was a disaster, and only he survived the ordeal. Nevertheless, he was always able to turn his follies into fantastic tales of adventure. I did get to see many wonderful places, though.

"How come nothing happened when he pointed you at the avalanche?"

I haven't always been able to do everything I can do now. And sometimes I didn't want to help those who wielded me.

"I have a feeling that every great event or person in history might have something to do with you."

I have been a part of some of the most wonderful things and some of the most abhorrent things anyone would care to imagine, but I haven't been a part of everything. At least, I don't think I have.

"It's said that Derrick Hitton's volumes fill a shelf in the great library in Rytin. I wonder if there is enough room there to hold all you have witnessed," he wondered aloud.

Bah, I didn't have much choice, but it matters not. What matters most is finding out what is creating these metal beasts.

"Indeed, you are right." The feeling of far-off danger still tugged at his senses. "Let's see if we can make some progress toward that end. I think this time I'll try a little less violent method to get us out."

He made his way to the wall of snow blocking the entrance and, using Lyn, began carefully melting away the snowy obstruction. It took nearly an hour of cutting packed snow to finally make it outside to the evening suns' light. Solar and Solis had passed below the peaks in the east, and the shadows from the multitude of mountains placed them in a premature night. Bright glittering stars filled the crisp clear sky, and the tops of the peaks appeared set ablaze by the light of the setting suns. The scene was breathtakingly beautiful. He stood with Vyckie there a moment to take it all in.

*   *   *

The Dread Lord's eye slits flared to life as he heard the distant thundering of an avalanche. He had been waiting out the storm for weeks. After a time, he could feel his prey beginning to move again. He raised his head and turned it in the direction of the Dread Commander armor worn by the imposter. The storm had passed, and he could now complete his master's task. Sitting atop the black drake, he commanded the dragon to wake.

Kharaxsis lay curled about the top of one of the many towering peaks.

They had waited out the ravaging storm high above the clouds. As he opened his eyes, Solar and Solis were setting in the east, and their red-orange glow illuminated the alabaster tops of the many mountains, making them look like flaming torches blazing in the darkening sky. The colorful display was lost on Kharaxsis and the Dread Lord, for they could not see color. The world to them was either black, white, or some shade of grey.

Kharaxsis unwound from the zenith and leapt into the thin air. His powerful wings spread wide as he dove down the steep slope. The rushing air whistled through his bristling horns as he gathered speed. His leathery wings creaked as wind rushed beneath him. It had been many weeks lying in wait. The Dread Lord pulled hard on the reins causing his neck to arch up and back, turning his dive up and away from the slope.

It was not hard to find the avalanche. Unlike all the nearby peaks, the entire mountaintop was devoid of snow. As the suns' light faded, he spotted the man and horse upon the snowy slope. Kharaxsis gave a cry as the Dread Lord drove him into a steep dive toward the two figures far below.

*   *   *

Vyckie and Tegain set out along the avalanched slope. Thankfully, the snow was densely packed which made traversing the mountainside a little easier than if the snow had just fallen. They had almost made it to the edge of the snow-slide when the hair on the back of Tegain's neck began to tingle. Something of great threat was close at hand. Confirming his suspicion, a piercing cry rang out from high above.

Forgetting for the moment the helm could enhance his sight, Tegain peered up into the starry sky with his normal vision. At first, he could only see the starry sky. By chance, he noticed a small void in the heavens where blackness was growing larger by the second. Soon the inky mass was blocking most of the glittering stars.

"Something is coming," he warned.

Hold me up!

He was already pulling her free from his back as she spoke. As he brought the blade up, a bolt of lightning arced from the tip of the glaive into the night sky. It streaked upward to illuminate the obsidian drake hurtling down from above. The dragon rolled to avoid the lancing bolt, causing it to veer from its intended target. The dragon unfolded its wings and pulled out of the dive at the last moment to crash heavily just behind them.

Vyckie needed no prompting to launch into a full gallop. Tegain was nearly tossed from his seat with the sudden burst of acceleration. He barely grasped a handful of mane as the sable steed sped away. A booming shriek from the enraged drake shook the mountainside. Tegain could hear the dragon taking wing as Vyckie plowed into the unpacked snow at the edge of the snow-slide. She slowed considerably in the deep drifts. Each step sank her all the way to her chest despite her oversized hooves.

"We are not going to be able to outrun it," said Tegain.

I know. I'm trying to think of something.

Tegain could feel the recovered dragon closing in from behind.

Let it catch you. With your armor, it shouldn't be able to hurt you, and that will allow Vyckie to get away. Then you can use me to make quick work of the beast.

Tegain quickly rolled from Vyckie's back to land in her wake. Before he could rise to his feet, he was ripped into the air. Heavy black-scaled claws held him tightly, binding his arms to his sides. Thankfully, he could still feel Lyn gripped in his right hand.

I can't move, thought Tegain as the dragon intensified its crushing hold. He struggled to breathe through the tortuous embrace. Armor buckled, and he felt his ribs cracking. "I can't last much longer," he pleaded as his vision constricted into a tunnel.

Using her connection through Tegain's mind, Lyn could feel by the position of his arms that she most likely protruded out past Tegain's feet. She only hoped it was beneath the dragon. *Hold me tight,* she commanded. Tendrils of power and light surged along the silvered glaive, building into a nimbus of energy at her tip. She released the blast in a halo from the apex of the blade. Punctuated by a powerful explosion, heat and light erupted from below the drake filling the night sky.

Tegain's vision went completely black. As he held the hilt fast, thunder boomed from what seemed far off in the distance. He felt the crushing cease and the pit of his stomach rise with the unmistakable feeling of falling. Several moments of grogginess clouded his thoughts as he plunged earthward on his back; his vision slowly returned to reveal the dark drake hurtling toward him from above. Fear of the terrifying sight of the chasing dragon almost stopped his heart. Strangely, the two red dots just above the dragon's horned head drew his attention.

Finally remembering the helm's ability, he directed it to focus on the ruby lights. Instantly, his vision magnified to show the drake's pitch-black rider. His armor resembled that of a Dread Knight, but it was slightly different. Though he appeared small compared to his mount, the rider was much larger than a normal man. As Tegain looked upon him with enhanced vision, the Dread Lord's crimson slits blazed with hatred.

"I thought all the Dread Knights were destroyed," wondered Tegain as he hurtled toward the earth.

That doesn't look like any Dread Knight I've ever seen, and especially not riding on something like that.

"What exactly is that?"

I'm not quite sure, but it isn't friendly. After all this time, I had thought he would have gone, she mused to herself, but somehow it slipped through their mental connection.

"Who's he?" said Tegain.

No time to explain. It looks like they're gaining on us. Let's not get caught again.

Bracing Lyn with both hands Tegain levelled her toward the oncoming dark figures. A flash of lightning flared from the tip of the two-handed blade. The bolt struck the beast on the left shoulder. Following the booming clap, the drake unfurled its bat-like wings to slow its descent. Beating furiously, the black-scaled beast came to a hover.

Tegain started to think this was a little too easy, as the sides of the crevasse appeared in the corners of his vision. The beast snarled and roared with frustration as it watched Tegain descend farther into the gorge. Red blazing slits flared above the drake's head, as Tegain continued to fall.

This is going to hurt, isn't it? thought Tegain. The rocky walls of the fissure blurred as he sank further into the abyss.

I will try— began Lyn as Tegain struck the water at bottom of the chasm.

*   *   *

Kharaxsis hovered for a moment to observe the false dread commander disappearing into the darkness of the fissure. He took some satisfaction that the offensive little man would be severely injured by the fall. Never had he felt such pain. The power of the blade was nothing he had ever experienced before. Pain from his abdomen and shoulder where the blade had struck throbbed with each beat of his wings. He would take greater care to avoid the sword if they met again.

If the Dread Lord had a mouth, its corners would have been drawn down. He was vexed. This false commander was proving to be troublesome. The storm had delayed the pursuit some weeks, and now this. Nothing the Dread Lord had done up until this point had taken this much patience. Nothing had been able to withstand him. Now, he would have to wait again until the irksome prey emerged from the chasm. So be it. It was only time. When next they met, he would take matters into his own hands.

*   *   *

As the obsidian drake hovered off in the distance, Vyckie knew that Tegain had escaped for the moment. The feeling of his presence dimmed as he fell into the chasm. She would follow that connection no matter the cost.

Six-striders had been paired with each Dread Commander. When the previous commander had been vanquished, that connection had been severed. Somehow, after she had blacked out from her chest wound, she had awakened in possession of a new body. Vyckie's desire to protect Tegain had drawn her into the powerful cyne that connected a Dread Commander to his steed.

CHAPTER 6

"The bigger they be; the more wee yer place o' hiding."

-Karl Dunmire

A thin line of white smoke drifted up from the Talenshan quarry. Guards patrolling along the western wall had seen the warning fire, and they had sounded the alarm bells. Captain Marshal Donaldson and Karl had been summoned. As they peered at the distant signal, Karl rubbed his dark goatee. He had been expecting this for quite some time now. It had been three long weeks since the arrival of the captain marshal. He only wondered what kind of threat the signal fire foretold.

If the metallic spiders were coming again, they still had no way of combating the horde. Kord had yet to make one of the light tubes create the fiery beam. He only hoped they had made enough reflectors. Even with the mirrors, Karl had no idea how they would destroy them.

Donaldson, to his left, looked eager for the coming peril. The fool had no idea the massacre that would befall them if it were truly the alien host. After the declaration of marshal law, the stunted marshal had assumed control of the city and its defenses. Despite Donaldson's best efforts, Karl was still able to contain most of the idiotic directives the captain marshal spawned on an almost daily basis. Donaldson seemed hell-bent on changing anything Karl had put in place before the captain marshal's arrival.

"I hope it is these… what did Master Kord call them?" wondered the runty captain marshal, as he peered out in the direction of the quarry.

"Myders," answered Karl.

"Yes, that was it! Myders… I wish to see them moving about," chirped Donaldson.

Karl lowered and shook his head in frustration. Under his breath, he said, "It be the last thing ye be seeing." As he raised his head, he said aloud, "I be hoping it be anything but that."

Donaldson harrumphed and frowned his displeasure at Karl's statement. "Come now, my man. I have an entire regiment of the king's finest Dragoons; we have nothing to fear."

This time it was Karl who harrumphed before he said under his breath, "Just means more be dying."

"What was that?" demanded Donaldson.

"I be wishing someone be cyning," said Karl.

The marshal tiptoed to peer farther over the bulwark as he spoke. "Thank the Nine they are all holed up in their tower. We have no need of their ilk."

Karl frowned heavily as he stared at the back of the stumpy marshal's head. A fleeting desire to toss the offensive man from the wall flashed in his mind. He let it go. Time had a way of dealing with people like him. Eventually, circumstances created through their own ineptitude brought about their downfall. Karl had lived long enough now to see it happen many times. If he could, he would try to lessen the devastation that was sure to come.

"I be not knowing a cynosure to ever be causing harm to anyone," said Karl. Crossing his arms across his chest, he tried to recall the last time he had seen a cynosure.

"No man should have that much power. It can only lead to misuse of it," declared Donaldson. He lowered himself from peering over the wall and looked to Karl. "If not for Kaerin Kabe, we would still be under their cyne. All of us slaves to their will and not even knowing it."

"That be one way o' looking at it," Karl said softly to himself. He didn't remember ever slaving under the will of a cynosure. It seemed to be quite the opposite, as he recalled. They all seemed very compassionate and kind. Now that he thought about it, something about learning to cyne seemed to make cynosures very selfless and loving. He didn't have time to contemplate further, as a trail of dust rose from the quarry road.

A lone rider sped toward Talenshan. Karl and Donaldson watched as the figure made his inexorable way to the gates. Light from the midday suns shone brightly, and only a few wispy clouds marred the otherwise clear blue sky.

"We be knowing soon," said Karl under his breath.

Both men made their way down off the wall to the western gate to meet the speeding rider. As the two large wooden gates swung open wide, the marshals could clearly see the mounted man racing up the road. Karl recognized the slender youth. Jarid was a newly minted dragoon who'd had barely a few weeks of training before being sent out with Donaldson's regiment. Apparently, Jarid had run away from home when he had seen a ball of light burn across the sky some months ago.

Lather covered the laboring steed as it came to a sliding stop just before the two men. The wide-eyed youth leapt from the back of the chestnut mare to land lightly on his feet.

"Ca… Captain Marshal," began Jarid, his speech broken by his heavy breathing. "Something, something is…"

"Spit it out, boy!" commanded Donaldson.

Jarid took in a deep, steadying breath before he spoke in a rush. "Something is coming down from the Hittons. They're riding six-legged bears. They're huge!"

"Sixton bears," breathed Karl. "Only one thing be riding sixton bears… rock reavers." Karl lowered his head, his lips pursed in concentration. "Now, I really be wishing we be having a cynosure," he muttered to himself.

"What do you know of these beasts?" asked Donaldson.

"Be the training so lacking these days in the Dragoons?"

Donaldson puffed up, taking sudden offense. "My men are the finest trained Dragoons. How dare you insult—"

Before the captain marshal's tirade gathered steam, Karl interrupted. "I be not insulting ye or your men. Be ye not training for every known foe?" Seeing the quizzical look on Donaldson's face, Karl added, "From the *Book of Legion* by Marshal Sanger. It be describing every known creature and its weakness."

Donaldson looked dumbstruck for a moment. "I would be laughed out of the Dragoons if I used that book to train anyone. Those creatures are just fairy tales to scare children…" he trailed off.

"Be that so?" said Karl as he stared out past Jarid toward the Hittons. "Best be getting the folk inside," he said to Jarid. "I be thinking we're in for a bit o' fighting." He looked to Donaldson with a grimace. "And we best be getting as many men as we can to the western wall."

Runners were sent out through the city to gather every able body to the city wall in defense. The gates were closed and barred. Donaldson and Karl made their way back to the top of the western wall to wait for the coming threat. It wasn't very long before the wisp of white smoke from the signal fire ceased and dust rose from the quarry road.

As they watched from the wall, Karl relayed to Donaldson what he knew of rock reavers and the sixton bears. From what he could remember from his training those many years ago, rock reavers were humanoid creatures with rock-hard skin. Their favored weapons were stones, which they hurled with great precision and power. Then there were the humungous six-legged bears they rode into battle. The sixton bears could stand up on their hind legs and attack the top of city walls up to twenty feet high. One swipe from their claws could send scores of men to their deaths. And their thick fur and hide protected them from heavy blows and even arrows.

Of course, they hadn't been seen in over two thousand years. Even Karl had never seen either of them in the flesh. He couldn't remember any special tactic for fighting them, only that they were very tough and none too bright. Hopefully, he would have a plan by the time they reached the city.

Jarid had been right in his assessment of the sixton bears. Indeed, they were humungous. Lumbering out of the dust from the quarry road, the bears were larger than any living thing Karl had ever seen. All he could think was, *What does something that big eat*? A horde of grey-skinned figures strode next to the three giant bears. The thin figures had curiously long arms. Karl knew they had to be as tall as or taller than a normal person. However, the reavers were barely knee high to the giant six-legged bears.

The men standing along the wall next to him were muttering, fear working its way into their minds. He would have to do something soon to keep them from thinking too much. Donaldson seemed oblivious to what needed to be done, staring in awe at the sixton bears.

A sharp crack resounded, and a puff of rock and dust sprayed off the merlon in front of them. Similar sounds echoed along the wall. Then the cries of injured and frightened men erupted in response. True to their name, the rock reavers were hurling rocks from ranges no bow could reach. They used their abnormally long arms in a strange whip-like motion that sent stones of various sizes with enough power to pulverize them against the city wall. Those unlucky enough to be hit with the missiles were knocked from their feet, never to rise again. The sight of those struck down was cause for much of the screaming.

"Get down!" ordered Karl as he grabbed Donaldson and pulled him down from the embrasure. The order was repeated down the line.

"Fascinating! Did you see the size of those things?"

"I be seeing."

"At least there were only three of them," said Donaldson.

"I be thinking one be more than enough," Karl said as the rain of shattering stones continued to pelt the wall. "We need to be getting everyone off the wall."

"But you just ordered everyone to the wall," scoffed Donaldson. "I'm beginning to think you don't know what you're doing."

"I be having a plan," said Karl. "Be needing to open the gates and be getting your best fighters to follow me. Everyone else be needing to get below to the sewers."

"Are you insane, my man? We can't open the gates and just let them in," gasped the captain marshal.

"Do ye be thinking the gates be holding against an assault by even one o' those beasties?" asked Karl. "Be better to leave the gates whole than let them be destroyed. I be intending to lead them into the catacomb of the city hall. I be thinking their rock tossing be for naught in tight spaces."

"I don't think that is a very good plan," said Donaldson.

Karl stood up behind a merlon. He reached down and dragged Donaldson by his lapels to his feet. "Do ye be having a better plan?" he asked, inches from Donaldson's face.

Donaldson looked fit to burst. He gritted his teeth as he hissed, "I won't let you lead my men anywhere. I am the one in charge here."

Karl released him and asked in a pleasant tone, "What be yer plan?"

Donaldson stood there for a moment contemplating. When an answer didn't seem forth coming, Karl prompted, "Well?"

"I... I... by the Nine you have a way about you that I just can't quite grasp. What you suggest seems best," admitted Donaldson. "But I will be going with you. I will have Major Roberts take charge of leading everyone into the sewers."

Karl frowned his agreement. He then called to Thom and Franc, who were crouched by a nearby merlon. After detailing the plan to the two swordsmen, he turned back to Donaldson. "Let's be going now. Time be a' wasting. Tell yer man to be getting everyone below. We be heading to open the gates."

"How many men do we need?" asked Donaldson.

"No more than twenty good men. I be having ten. Be getting your ten and meet me in the city square in front of the city hall," directed Karl, and he made his way down the steps to the western gate. Thom and Franc followed close behind.

On the way to the western gate, Karl turned to Thom. "Be getting Jeri and the others and be meeting me in the square. Franc and me be taking care of the gate."

"Aye, Captain Marshal. See you soon," replied Thom, peeling away to fetch Jeri and the others.

"Be getting below, boys—quickly now," said Karl. He and Franc made their way through the soldiers leaving the wall. They arrived at the western gate to see it still barred and guarded.

The rock reavers had ceased hurling stones, and the walls had grown eerily quiet with the men's withdrawal. Karl ordered, "Ye be needing to unbar and open the gates," clearly startling the men standing sentry.

"But those things are coming," said the nearest soldier.

"That's precisely why we be needing to open this here gate," said Karl. "Ye be needing to get below to the sewers. It be futile to be trying to stop what's coming. Better to let 'em in and be fighting where they be at a disadvantage."

"If you say so," said the guard. "All right, lads, you heard the city marshal. Let's get this gate open."

"Hurry now," said Karl. "Time be slipping away."

It took all five guards plus Karl and Franc to remove the large, iron-bound beam barring the gate. Once the brace was set to the side, they raised the portcullis. As the wheel to the winch was locked in place, a low, guttural growl rumbled from somewhere not too far outside the gates.

"Okay, boys. I be thinking it be time fer ye to go," Karl said to the guards.

"What about you?" asked a soldier.

"Someone needs to be showing these beasties where to go," replied Karl. "Go now!"

The guards hurried off as Karl and Franc took up a position in the fairway leading to the city center. It wasn't long before the booming of footfalls could be heard. Franc looked nervously at Karl as they stood in the middle of the roadway.

Standing resolute and calm, Karl waited patiently for what was to come through the gate. He had a moment to wonder why they were under attack from this new foe. The myders must be causing all these beasties to flee their homes in the Hittons.

After seeing the rock reavers and sixton bears in the flesh, he could see they were deadly in wide open spaces, but if he could get them into the tight confines of the newly transformed city hall, then the twists and turns could be used to negate almost all their advantage. It was just a matter of getting them into the catacombs.

A deep, booming roar emanated over the city walls as the host approached just outside the western gates.

"Shouldn't we take some cover?" said Franc.

"Aye, but they be needing to be seeing us first," said Karl.

With a deafening crash, the two massive iron gates were flung back against their thrusts. Filling the space created by the open gates stood the hulking sixton bear. From this distance, it seemed unbelievable. Only its head and some of its shoulders fit into the twenty-foot-tall and fifteen-foot-wide opening. It lunged forward and let loose a powerful roar. The city wall shook from the sudden assault. Even the ground reverberated with the beast's bellow.

"I think they be seeing us," said Karl.

"I hope so," said Franc.

"Be following me lead."

Karl sprinted for the closest building to the north as stones from the reavers whizzed past them. He dove into the doorway, with Franc landing roughly next to him.

"Are ye all right?" asked Karl.

"I think so," replied Franc.

"Damn, those be some stone-hurling fiends."

"I couldn't agree more."

Karl jumped to his feet and helped Franc to his. The front windows shattered as more missiles were launched their way. "Out the back," said Karl, and he made his way through what appeared to be left of a fabric shop. They entered the cramped alleyway between the rows of buildings.

"We be not wanting to be staying here long," declared Karl.

"Where to?" asked Franc.

"East," said Karl. He hurried farther along the alley to the next doorway. Franc followed at his heels.

They entered the storage area of what looked like some kind of eatery. Hurrying through the kitchen and the dining area, the two men found themselves back out in the main thoroughfare. Franc dared a glance toward the breached city gate. Several rock reavers still stood at its mouth. He could also see a sixton bear climbing over the thirty-foot wall as the reavers took aim at them.

"Be looking to where ye want to go," warned Karl.

A stone ripped past Franc's head. Ducking low, he raced after Karl as more stones whizzed past them. Rushing headlong, they entered a high-end clothing shop. They found their way to the back and out into the alley in short order. Karl proceeded to head east and into the next building, then again across the main avenue in zigzag fashion until they reached the city square.

Captain Marshal Donaldson, Jeri, and several men stood ready at the city fountain as Franc and Karl burst through the alleyway into the square.

"Follow me," Karl called to the waiting men. He sprinted to the shell of the city hall. Before they could even enter the safety of the building, a hail of stones burst all around them.

"Now what?" demanded Donaldson.

"Now, the fun be beginning."

CHAPTER 7

"Fear… it can take so many delectable forms. I love to play with them all."

-Hael Atos

Through the eyes of his minion, Hael had watched Tegain plummet into the abyss between the towering peaks. Sensing the vexation of the Dread Lord, he smirked and let slip what seemed to be a laugh. Lifting his head from the pillow and opening his eyes, he peered about his lavishly adorned bedroom. None of his slaves seemed to have been disturbed. Well, that was unexpected, he thought after a moment had passed. What fun. Nothing in centuries had been able to elicit his laughter.

His thoughts focused on the glaive that had fallen with the false commander. This sword was truly a wonder. He had not witnessed such power in eons. Indeed, it must possess a soul, but who could have created it? Galesh and his rabble had been defeated ages ago. In all his attempts to imbue inanimate objects with a soul, none could do what he saw this sword doing. Whose soul was it? Hael needed to know. He would have to obtain this blade.

Before he ceased the mental link to his Dread Lord, Hael punished him for losing the opportunity to acquire the sword. Closing his eyes again, he drifted off, dreaming of what he would do once he acquired the weapon.

*　　*　　*

Agony exploded in the mind of the dark rider. Every fiber in his being was on fire. Torment rocked him forward in his seat, and he swooned against the slender neck of the soaring drake.

It was some time before he could clear his thoughts. No words were necessary from the master. The degree of pain expressed his anger. Many times, he had seen others suffer the master's displeasure, but never had he been the direct recipient of such dissatisfaction. At least, he was alive.

Kharaxsis circled higher as he waited for his rider to revive. When he had recovered enough to sit up, the Dread Lord directed Kharaxsis to the west, where there appeared to be an end to the long, narrow ravine. The black drake banked hard to the left. As he came about, his wings were nearly perpendicular to the earth. He levelled out and shot down to the west. Finding a suitable place to enter the crevasse turned out to be impossible. The slender seam between the crags ended abruptly in the middle of a snow-covered mountainside. The Dread Lord dismounted and stood at the start of the fissure. From the edge of the deep drop, he could hear the far-off rush of water echoing up from the blackness.

Confident that the false commander could not scale the sheer cliffs from this direction, he remounted and flew to the east to find the far end of the ravine. Finally, after several hours, the crevasse widened, and the walls dropped low enough to allow him easy access to the chasm. Here he dismounted and commanded Kharaxsis to wait for his return. Using his powerful hind legs, the black drake leapt into the night air and soared off to wait for his rider's call.

The Dread Lord turned to the stream's raging waters. The white water seemed to swallow the obsidian figure whole as he waded out into the torrent. Unfazed by the pounding flow, the Dread Lord proceeded to the center of the river. Reaching its middle, he turned and advanced against the rush toward the false commander.

*   *   *

Vyckie came to the edge of the ravine where Tegain had fallen. Hours passed in the twilight glow as she struggled through the heavy snow on her way to him. She could feel him far below in the depths. He had not moved in the time that it had taken to reach him. Sensing his armor repairing his broken body, she knew he was barely alive. From the ledge, there appeared to be no path on which to travel to the bottom, and it might take days to find a way if there even was one. Part of the cyne that had created her continually compelled her to be by his side. Due to the power of her connection to Tegain and his armor, the sable mare paced the edge of the crevasse in frustration.

Torn between staying or finding a way down, Vyckie decided to wait. For now, this was as close as she could get to him. If he did not move by morning, she would venture out to find a way down. Vyckie stopped patrolling the precipice and halted to begin a vigil over Tegain, who lay deep within the bowels of the chasm. As the cold of the night hours began to set in, she reluctantly forced herself into the hibernation state she had used in the weeks of solitude in the tiny mountainside shelter.

The cyne-created mare possessed the unique ability to control every function of her physical form. Slowing her metabolism, she enabled herself to reduce her heartrate to only a single beat an hour. Each breath was so gradual, it took even longer for a single respiration. Sustaining the giant steed were six cyne-forged horseshoes. These finely crafted crescents meshed seamlessly with her hooves. Much like a piezoelectric effect, her shoes generated renewing energy to her as pressure was applied through them. Consequently, she felt immeasurable exhilaration while running. Being in motion renewed her body and made her feel incredibly invigorated. When she was human, Vyckie had despised running, but now she found it hard to just stand still.

Nighttime slipped into dawn as Solar and Solis rose, and still Tegain had not moved. Vyckie shook the windblown snow from her flanks and stamped her hooves in the deep, drifted snow. She carefully leaned her head out over the abyss to try to catch a glimpse of him. However, she could only see blackness in the depths. With great regret, Vyckie turned from the side of the ravine and charged off to the east to find a way to reach him.

*   *   *

Tegain lay on the bottom of the riverbed. His powerful armor sustained him even in the murky depths. The impact from hitting the surface had crushed his body and knocked him unconscious. Still gripping the hilt of Lyn, he dreamed. They were not nightmares of loss and pain from his past, but of Lyn. She had come to him as she had been all those millennia before becoming a sword. Time slowed, moments measured in eons. Never had Tegain beheld such beauty. A halo of red-gold hair framed Lyn's delicate features. Her steel-grey eyes held him enraptured. In the depths open to him through the windows of her soul, he lost himself. Wisdom and knowledge swirled with patience and compassion. And then she smiled, a slight lifting at the corners of her mouth. To see her smile set his soul ablaze; he desired only to remain here with her.

Slowly, her pleased look transformed into a frown, and Tegain's joy turned to heartache. He would do anything to make her smile once again.

Lyn spoke softly. "Wake up, Tegain."

"But, why? I am here with you…" he trailed off with a pleading look.

"It is but a dream."

"I know, but I… I would rather stay here with you."

Lyn lowered her eyes, lost in thought for a brief moment, and then returned her gaze to his. "I know," she whispered softly. "But this is not the place, and this is not the time." With an upraised hand, she tenderly touched his cheek. Light and fire exploded into Tegain's vision as power flowed into his body from Lyn's caressing palm. "Please, Tegain awake! Something approaches."

Power and light flashed again as his vision of Lyn faded. He opened his eyes to darkness and pain. It took him a moment to realize where he was. Rushing water rippled and swirled around him and several boulders at the bottom of a riverbed.

Lyn called out in his mind over the gushing flow, *Hurry, Tegain. Your armor senses danger nearby.*

"How long was I—"

Lyn cut him off, *At least a day. Please, Tegain we must move. If it is the dark rider, I do not think we can stand against him.*

Through the pain and confusion, Tegain felt the unmistakable dread produced by the armor's warning. He struggled to his feet as torrents of water pushed and pulled him seemingly in all directions. *How could something be coming through this?* he thought.

Something I do not wish to battle with you in your current state. I also cannot use my power in the water without hurting you, too.

"Where should I go?"

Let's try and get above the water; at least then I can be more effective.

Tegain slowly crept along the riverbed perpendicular to the flow. Using Lyn to help keep his feet, he eventually reached the side of the chasm. Here the rush of water was weaker than in the center. Climbing the cliff would be an altogether different challenge. Sheer, slime-covered rock walls provided no means of purchase.

Bracing himself between some boulders at the base of the wall, he carefully cut several handholds into the solid stone. Creeping dread rose in the pit of his stomach as he worked the blade to fashion a means for his escape. When enough holes were created, he began to climb as quickly as he could manage in the flow. More than once, his hand or foot was torn from its tenuous hold by the torrential waters. Only his firm grip on Lyn's hilt kept him from being ripped from the wall.

Fear and dread fueled his racing heart. Every slip and misstep sent him further into a panic. Soon the pounding of his own heart drowned out the crashing flow, and he stopped moving. He could feel that whatever was approaching was very close.

Tegain, Lyn called over the drumming. *Where are you?*

It took a moment to register what she was asking. "I… I don't know where I am," he responded through gritted teeth. "Why does it matter!"

You are not here. It is the only thing that matters. Your fear is keeping you from the present moment. Right here and right now should be the only things that concern you. Fear is an emotion to help you focus. Use it to focus on what is important. You are here and now.

Tegain clung to the precipitous wall and took in a deep, calming breath. His thoughts had been anything other than in the present moment. Lyn was right, of course. Starting out once more, as he climbed he kept a mantra in his mind: *I am here. I am now.*

Breaching the raging waters, Tegain found his way becoming easier. However, he took no notice. He continued with purpose up the sheer cliff. Feelings of dread still hovered about him, but they no longer controlled him. Instead, he used his fear-heightened senses to his advantage. No longer dwelling on what was coming, he intently focused on the present moment. As a result, he rose up the cliff at a steady, measured pace.

Water still dripped from Tegain's armor when the pitch-black helm of the Dread Lord appeared from the depths of the raging torrent just below him. Glowing red slits flared brightly as they beheld their prey. Tegain hazarded a glance below to the figure rising from the stream. The dark warrior's eye slits blazed red, and his armor was so devoid of light that he seemed unearthly.

Ascending the vertical face, the Dread Lord appeared not to struggle in the slightest against the river's powerful current. Tegain saw immediately that he could not outpace the coming foe.

"He is going to catch me."

Is that so?

"Unless you have something in mind."

Indeed, I do. Point me at him.

Holding fast to the wall, Tegain levelled Lyn toward the oncoming threat. White hot energy flared from the tip of the glaive and arced down upon the obsidian giant. The energy bore into the figure, who seemed to absorb the power. The burst of light and heat dissipated as instantly as it had arrived. With its collapse, a wave of heat and sound blasted from the epicenter around the dark figure.

Where once clung an obsidian man, there was now empty space. Steam still rose from the turbulent waters, and the cliff face glowed red with the intense heat, so violent had been the force of the blast.

There, I think that should do it, said Lyn from out of the ringing din.

"I would hope so." Looking down to the turbulent waters, Tegain hoped that was the end of the pursuit. When the white water revealed nothing, he turned back to scaling the side of the ravine. Hours passed in supreme concentration as he ascended the near sheer wall. Midday light faded to premature dusk, and still he had not reached the top of the precipice.

"By the Nine, does this ever end?" Tegain cursed to the unending cliff.

Getting to the top will only be the beginning.

"Aye, I know. At least Vyckie is safe," Tegain whispered under his breath. He could feel the sable mare far off to the east. She must have gone in search of a way down to him. He took some comfort in her having escaped harm. For some reason he felt drained, despite the power of the living armor.

"It's probably safer that she not be near us."

I agree, but I highly doubt she feels the same. I think she would give her life for you again without a second thought.

"I know you are right. And it is for that reason alone I wish her to be safe. She has given so much already."

Again, I agree. She has given much, but who are you to say she cannot give any more? How would you feel if your offer were refused? Seldom does giving to others seem balanced. However, there is much we do not see.

Clinging to the cliffside, Tegain felt overwhelmed. "I know what you say is true. It is just that I… I feel I am not worthy of what has been given."

Is that so? Who would be worthy then? Is one man more worthy than another? He started to respond. However, she continued, *Who assigned this worth? Do all creatures great and small subscribe to your sense of worth? Or is all that exists just as it should be?* Lyn paused a moment to let Tegain consider. *No, you are not worthy, and neither are you unworthy. But, surely, you must know by now the power of your thoughts. Let this feeling of not deserving go. You are the one creating it.*

If only it were that simple to change your mind, thought Tegain.

Really, scoffed Lyn. *It can be, but I know what you mean. At least, now you are aware that you are creating the thought. This in and of itself gives it less sway over you.*

After a moment, he agreed, "Aye, I feel you are right." Feeling better, he let his thoughts turn back to the here and now as he began to climb again. With his fear gone, he was finding climbing to be very enjoyable. It definitely kept him in the present moment. Any stray thought caused him to miss a hold or slow his ascent. However, with his mind clear and focused, time seemed not to pass, and he climbed steadily higher.

Unexpectedly, while thrusting Lyn up to cut the next handhold, Tegain encountered nothing but empty space. Placing Lyn on his back, he reached up to grasp the unseen ledge. Carefully, he pulled himself up into what appeared to be quite a large cave in the side of the cliff wall.

"Hmm, I didn't see this on the way down. Of course, I don't think I was looking at the sides at the time," he commented.

I missed it as well. This cave is definitely not natural either. There seems to be some kind of coating on the walls.

Tegain walked over to the nearest wall to get a closer look. Indeed, a black substance seemed to have been glazed over everything. "Strange, I wonder what this stuff is?" he wondered aloud as he touched the hardened dark material.

I'm not sure. But, I have a feeling whatever lives here probably won't like us traipsing about its doorstep.

"True. But, I think these tunnels are abandoned."

How do you know that?

"There's no warning from the suit."

Well, yes, I guess we could assume so. Or maybe we just haven't aroused its ire.

"Aye, and I don't plan on arousing anyone's ire, either. I would like to rest for a bit, though. For some reason, I feel exhausted from the climb."

I think you may still be recovering from your fall. I feel the armor does have some limits. We should try and be more careful.

"I couldn't agree more. I certainly didn't expect to be dropped from the sky by a huge flying lizard ridden by a giant knight," said Tegain.

Indeed, the dark knight and his mount were quite formidable.

"That reminds me, you were going to tell me more about this Hael fellow," prompted Tegain.

Yes, I guess now is as a good a time as any. Sit and rest, and I will tell you what I can remember.

Tegain sat with his back to the cavern wall and placed Lyn across his lap. Once he was settled, Lyn began to tell of Hael Atos. Much of what she knew of him came from stories she had heard growing up. Long before she had finished her tale, Tegain drifted off to sleep

CHAPTER 8

"Ye truly be not knowin' a man till ye be in combat. Then ye be knowin' all ye be needin' to know."

-Karl Dunmire

Stones pinged and popped outside the blackened catacomb as Karl, Donaldson, and the other men took cover away from the entrance. Karl counted only fourteen men huddled on either side of the broken doorway. It would have to be enough. At least, Thom had found Jeri and had made it to the rendezvous in the square. In fact, most of the faces were familiar. Donaldson had only managed to bring three of his men.

"Where be the rest o' your men?" Karl asked Donaldson, who crouched to the side of the now silent opening across from him.

"Lieutenant Scott should be coming shortly with the rest of my men," said Donaldson.

Karl hazarded a quick glance out into the city square. Whipping his head back behind cover, a fresh hail of stones ricocheted into the hallway where his head had just been.

"By the Nine," breathed Karl as he felt the rush of bullets zip past his ear. His quick glance had only given him enough time to evaluate the enemies' position. They were not advancing and seemed to be preparing to take up firing positions from the back of the city center. There was no way Lieutenant Scott would make it safely to them.

"Yer men not be coming," observed Karl when the echo of exploding rocks died.

"Yes, they will."

"If they be having any sense, they be staying out o' the square."

"My men will do what I have ordered them to do."

"By the Nine." Karl shook his head as he contemplated how to keep Scott and his men from being slaughtered. However, before he could formulate anything, a deep, rumbling growl reverberated out in the square, and a heavy staccato of footfalls thudded closer. "Move!" warned Karl.

Darkness enveloped the entrance as the men scrambled to get farther into the catacomb. The enormous head of the sixton bear filled the entryway just before the entire catacomb shook from the beast's impact. Karl and the men involuntarily cringed and covered their ears from the deafening roar that followed.

"By the Nine." Momentarily deaf, Karl glanced back at the massive snout that bristled with teeth the size of a man's arm. "By the Nine, that be one big beastie."

The sixton bear roared again, sweeping its head from side to side in an attempt to reach the fleeing men. Once he felt he was out of reach, Karl stopped and turned back to observe the creature filling the entrance. A giant pitch-black orb gazed back at him with wild rage. Its brow furrowed as it growled. Karl noticed scorch marks and cuts all along the bear's snout. It let loose another thundering cry, this time directed at Karl. A blast of hot, foul breath assaulted him. His eyes watered, and he nearly gagged.

Before he could clear his stinging eyes, the bear had retreated from the entrance. Light flooded the space once occupied by the massive head. After a few booming strides, the entire catacomb began to shudder from heavy blows directly above his position. In between impacts, the unsettling sound of scraping from giant claws resounded through the hallway.

From across the entrance, Karl saw Donaldson staring at him with a questioning look. There was no way Karl could be heard over the bear's onslaught. All he could do was gesture to Donaldson and his men to move farther back away from the entrance. Hopefully, the current captain marshal could figure out how to combat the rock reavers in the tunnels of the transformed city hall. From the befuddled look on Donaldson's face, Karl had a sinking feeling he would not fare well.

Fortunately, the former den of the vilekin seemed to be holding up well to the assault of the ferocious beast. However, Karl did not want to be in the vicinity of the walls if they did give way. He, Thom, Franc, Jeri, and the rest of the soldiers from Fulsom pushed back down the passage to the first intersection. They took up positions out of sight from the dimly lit main corridor and waited for the rock reavers to come to them.

They did not have to wait very long before the whiz of speeding stones could be heard over the pummeling from the sixton bear. Karl stood at the closest corner to the main entrance. Looking back at the shadowed faces of the men, he gave them a reaffirming nod and a knowing grin. Franc, Thom, and the others began to take up their positions along the hallway. His plan was simple. He and Jeri would be the decoy to draw the reavers' attention and lead them farther into the hall's depths. Once the bait was taken, the dragoons would ambush from the many rooms along its length.

With everyone in place, Karl checked with Jeri one last time. Jeri nodded his assent. Karl unlimbered his slender blade and brandished it out in the main hallway. Instantly, bullets began filling the space. As he withdrew the blade, it was struck by a speeding stone. The force of the impact nearly wrenched the rapier from his hand. Wincing in pain, he clutched his numb sword arm. Thankfully, his blade had not shattered from the blow.

"That be doing it. Let's be moving," said Karl.

"I see that," said Jeri as he turned to dash deeper into the hall.

Sprinting the entire length of the dark corridor, the two soldiers were out of breath when they stopped at the last intersection.

"Could you do me a favor?" asked Jeri between huffs.

"What be that?" asked Karl.

"Remind me to take ambush duty instead of decoy duty," said Jeri.

"Bah, ye be missing out on all the fun."

Looking back to check the opening, Karl and Jeri witnessed a rock reaver materialize from the shadowy space. Its head nearly touched the eight-foot ceiling, and yet its hands still almost dragged the ground. The hand itself was nearly as long as its upper arm. Everything about the creature seemed stretched to abnormal proportions. Its eyes were the only exception. Tiny red-glowing orbs were set deep into dark sockets. Thin greyish skin covered the creature, making it appear much like stone. Had it been standing in the rocks of the Hittons, it would have been almost invisible.

The beast had to hunch slightly to begin its attack. It folded its forearm up, the hand collapsing back flat against the rising arm. As the elbow reached horizontal, the folded forearm was perfectly level against the top of the extended upper arm. So long was its forearm that the folded hand lay fully behind the shoulder. With unbelievable agility, the arm whipped down, and the limb uncoiled to send a stone hurtling toward them at a deadly velocity.

Jeri and Karl each dove to opposite sides of the passageway as the bullet exploded on the wall behind them. Taking defensive positions against the wall, they looked to each other.

Karl cracked a grin. "See what I be meaning?"

"Not really," replied Jeri, shaking his head slightly while trying to suppress a chuckle.

The shuffling of feet came from along the hallway. Karl could feel his body getting ready for battle. The pit of his stomach dropped, and his chest tightened. He welcomed the invigorating surge of energy. More scraping footfalls filled the air as they waited for the closest beast to breach their position.

Karl could hear the reaver just beyond his spot suddenly stop. Long, grey fingers unexpectedly appeared from around the corner, and hard, grey nails clicked down inches from his face. As the head of the creature came into view, Karl readied his blade. He quickly thrust his rapier into the eye of the surprised reaver. The beast was instantly slain.

"Dragoons," called Karl, as the reaver collapsed into a heap at his feet. He and Jeri entered the passageway at a dead run. With the signal given, the waiting soldiers sprang from their hiding places to assault the unsuspecting rock reavers. Even at close range, the reavers strange, whip-like arms were still lethal.

Rounding the corner into the dimly lit passage, Karl immediately confronted the next reaver. It lashed out with its unique arms, using them like whips and flailing at the two assailants. Ear-splitting pops punctuated each strike. Keeping their distance, Jeri and Karl kept the beast's attention focused on them. Hearing similar whip-cracks coming from behind, he knew their comrades would not be able to help in time.

After several strikes, Karl noticed a pattern. The reaver seemed to be attacking with only one arm at a time. When it switched to strike with the opposite arm, the beast had to shift its feet and weight slightly to compensate for the power of the blow. This left a fraction of a second between each strike.

Apparently, the beast could not attack with both arms at once.

"Are ye seeing what I be seeing?" Karl asked without taking his eyes from the reaver.

"Aye," replied Jeri.

"Next one," said Karl.

Finishing its onslaught on Jeri, the reaver shifted and struck out toward Karl. Air cracked, and he moved to attack. Unable to defend or strike, the fiend cried out in a shrill whine as Karl's sword struck him in the gut. He quickly sprang back to avoid a counterattack; however, Karl could see he had taken the fight out of the creature.

Holding its belly, the reaver crumpled to the floor and whimpered pitifully. Karl didn't have time to feel sorry for it. His men were still fighting for their lives down the hall. They stepped over the mortally wounded creature, and Jeri ended its misery with a single blow.

Employing their newfound tactic, Jeri and Karl helped the remaining men dispatch the rest of the reavers with relative ease. However, several men had been severely injured during the brief melee. Twelve reavers had been downed, and three dragoons were too injured to fight despite their pleas to the contrary.

Shortly after the fray, the sixton bear had stopped its assault, and the tunnels had become eerily quiet. "Be readying yourselves men. More be coming for sure," said Karl.

The soldiers hurriedly ditched the reaver corpses into the many side rooms and prepared for the next wave of fiends. Jeri and Karl stood sentry at the entrance to their passageway. Time passed slowly as they waited for the reavers to make their next move.

In the moment of peace, he wondered how Captain Marshal Donaldson had weathered the reaver assault. Karl hoped that he and his men had taken the brunt of the attack, but there would be no way to know until the siege ended. His musings were interrupted by the shuffling of feet coming down the passageway.

The next wave of reavers was put down with no losses from the dragoon ranks. Bolstered by their recent success, they took down the following waves of reavers. With regularity, wave after wave came. True to what Karl had recalled, the reavers were not too bright tactically, but what they lacked in strategy they made up for in numbers. Solis and Solar had set in the east, and darkness had taken hold of the city, and still reavers came steadily to the waiting soldiers.

Once it became too dark to see, Karl had set up the stored lanterns at strategic points along the path of ambush. They were running out of room to stash the corpses accruing from the onslaught when, finally, it seemed the siege ended for the night. Karl felt it was sometime past midnight.

"I be thinking we be having a break," declared Karl after a new surge of reavers failed to appear after some time.

A half-muttered, "Aye," echoed back from the men hiding along the passageway.

"Rest where ye be," ordered Karl. "Jeri and I be taking the first watch. Mayhap they be out o' beasties to be sending," he added quietly.

"I hope you're right," said Jeri who sat across the hallway. "I'm glad that six-legged monster of a bear stopped trying to cave the place in. I wonder why it stopped."

"I think they be fighting scared. Their bear be showing signs o' myder attack," shared Karl. "If I be a betting man, there be myders coming soon."

"By the Nine," cursed Jeri. "I think I'd rather face the bear than those things. They make my skin crawl watching them skittering about."

"Aye, and all we be having are shiny discs and simple swords. I not be liking our chances," said Karl.

"I don't suppose you have a plan to fight those?" asked Jeri.

"Hide! Mayhap, some be surviving. They be moving too quick and those fiery tubes be deadly."

"Speaking of deadly, do you think the captain marshal is still alive?" wondered Jeri.

Karl chuckled to himself before he replied, "I'll not be surprised if he be finding some way o' surviving. His type always be finding a way."

The scraping of metal on stone halted their conversation. Karl and Jeri looked at each other as they waited for further confirmation.

"Hail! Anyone left alive?" called a soldier, stepping into the entrance of the catacomb. Karl recognized the man as Lieutenant Scott. It seemed he did have some sense about him.

"Aye, we be living," answered Karl.

"By the Nine, I had hoped as much after so many of those things had disappeared into here," said the lieutenant. "How many of you are left? Is Captain Marshal Donaldson among you?"

Jeri and Karl rose to their feet and moved to greet the lieutenant. "There be ten of us. Captain Donaldson not be one," replied Karl.

Scott let out an audible sigh of relief. "He'd have my head for not coming sooner, but I lost so many men trying to reach the entrance that I thought it best to wait."

"I be thinking ye made the right decision," said Karl. "But ye be not out o' the woods yet, Lieutenant. He may still be breathing somewhere on the other side of the passage." Karl pointed along the hallway behind Scott. "What be changing to clear the way?"

A worried look passed over the lieutenant's face as he responded, "They left… All at once they just picked up and headed out of the city."

"Which direction?" asked Jeri.

"To the east, toward Fulsom," answered the lieutenant.

Jeri and Karl shared a brief, knowing glance. "By the Nine," said Karl. "I be thinking as much."

"Only a matter of time before they get to Crossroads," said Jeri.

"Aye, and then to Rytin. There's no way Crossroads be faring well when all their troops be here."

"By the Nine," whispered Jeri. "I was hoping to take a break."

"Aye, be time enough for resting when ye be dead and buried. Let's be gathering the men. There be more fighting left to do." Jeri nodded and set off to do as he was directed. Karl turned to Lieutenant Scott. "It be not safe here.

Myders be coming. Everyone needs to be leaving this place."

"Everyone needs to leave?" asked Scott.

"Aye, be telling Captain Brent to be readying for evacuation. He be knowing what to do. I be going to see what be happening to the captain marshal."

"Aye, Captain," said Lieutenant Scott. He saluted and quickly exited the catacombs.

Karl bent low, grabbed the nearest lit lantern, and proceeded down the darkened corridor where he had last seen the captain marshal. Traversing several passageways, he had not encountered any sign of the marshal or reavers. However, after several more twists and turns, he came upon the bodies of three men. He could tell they were battered and bruised from close combat with the reavers.

Throughout the time, he called out into the darkness, "All be clear—it be safe to be coming out." There was no response to his call. Slowly, Karl made his way back to the entrance, repeating his call of all clear. He had almost given up hope when Donaldson suddenly materialized out of the darkness.

His eyes were wild with fear. "You deserted me," said Donaldson.

"I be doing nothing o' the sort," said Karl. The odor of urine and feces assaulted his senses as the captain marshal drew close to his face.

"You left me and my men to die!"

"There be no way to get to ye," began Karl, even though he knew there would be no way to reason with the deranged captain marshal.

"I saw you. You could have sent help after the bear," argued Donaldson, spittle flying from his lips.

"I be needing to prepare for the next attack."

"I declare a court martial against you and Lieutenant Scott for abandoning a commander in the field of battle," said Donaldson.

"Be that so?"

"I'll have your head on a pike for this," raged the captain marshal. "I should have never let you go as far as you have. You have no idea what you're doing."

"I be thinking ye'll find no one be truly knowing what they be doing. We all be doing the best we can with what we know."

Unfortunately, his wisdom was lost on the enraged captain marshal. Donaldson stomped off in a fury, screaming random names and orders as he went. Karl shook his head. He had seen this before. Donaldson would return tomorrow in a much more subdued mood. He might apologize for not being himself, or he might not even acknowledge what had occurred. Either way, Karl hoped the notion of a court martial would be dropped. There was no time to deal with such nonsense with all that needed to be done.

Karl knew why such men seemed to always end up in leadership positions. Men that could get the job done were left to do so. Those who kept getting in the way were promoted away from the front lines. This seemed to happen most often during long periods of peace. Nevertheless, peace was at an end. Men like Donaldson would have to be cleared from the field before too many had to pay with their lives.

CHAPTER 9

Trapped in the mountains cold

He descended into the deeper dark

Where terrors dwell from tales of old

He was sure to leave his mark

Carrying the blade of soul

Down, down into the deeper dark

He alone faced foes untold

-excerpt from *The Tale of Tegain*

The click of metal on stone echoed softly through the blackened cave entrance. Something prodded Tegain from his dreamy slumber. Initially, he barely opened his eyes. However, the vision of two red slits rising into the starry opening of the cave made his eyes pop wide open. Tegain hoped he was dreaming. When Lyn spoke, those hopes were crushed.

How did we not feel him coming?

"I don't know, but he's here."

Standing in the entrance, the Dread Lord's towering form voided the night sky behind him. Tegain gulped involuntarily. The obsidian knight's eye slits flared, and he reached back to unlimber his massive two-headed battle-axe. Now Tegain's suit gave warning of impending threat.

"I guess he wasn't intending harm until now," said Tegain.

I guess that makes sense.

"That axe is bigger than me," said Tegain as the Dread Lord brought his weapon to bear.

Oh my, you might want to stay out of the way of that thing.

Planting his trunk-like legs in a wide stance, the Dread Lord swung the man-sized axe as if he were hewing a tree. Air whistled as the huge weapon sliced toward Tegain. Still seated against the cavern wall, Tegain simply dropped to his side to avoid the blow. The black metal axe-head sank up to the shaft in the stone above him with an impact that seemed to shake the whole mountain.

He looked up at the lodged weapon, the pit of his stomach dropped out and fear blossomed in its place.

Stay with me.

"I can't fight that," Tegain said as he tried to scramble to his feet.

We don't have much of a choice.

"I barely know how to swing a sword without cutting myself. I'm doomed."

With one hand, the armored giant simply pulled the battle-axe from the wall and readied to swing again. A glowing red gash was left in the side of the tunnel.

Seeing the marred wall, Tegain thought, *I think he can kill me.*

Yes. I can see that. Clear your mind as if you're going to cyne. I'm going to try something. Hold on!

Time shifted as Lyn accelerated Tegain's metabolism, and suddenly the Dread Lord seemed to be moving in molasses. As he let go of his thoughts, the sound of his expelling breath drowned out all other noise. And then he began to move. With his mind clear, Lyn had assumed control of his body.

When she had been a princess, Lyn had practiced swordplay, and she had attained some degree of skill. However, after centuries of watching herself being wielded by knights, kings, and scoundrels, she was now a master in her own use. Over the ages, she had even developed some sword routines that only a vorpal blade like her could perform.

No longer controlling his body, Tegain could still see, hear, and feel everything taking place. Watching as Lyn blocked the coming attack, he felt her shift his feet slightly apart and bend his legs to absorb the coming blow. But even with augmented agility, it looked as though she might not be able to meet the attack.

Silence reigned in the time between the beat of his heart and the instant before the two weapons came together. Light flared, and a thunderous boom shook the cavern as the soul-forged battle-axe and sword met inches from his face. Created with similar properties, the two cyne-powered weapons reacted violently when they touched. A blast wave of superheated air and light erupted from the epicenter of their impact.

The force of the explosion rocked Tegain back on his heels and broke his concentration.

That was unexpected.

Tegain shook his head to clear the ringing in his ears as he replied, "Indeed." Across from him, the staggering Dread Lord shook his head as well. Dust and debris filled the air. "Let's not do that again."

Hmm. I think it may be because the edges touched. I will try to block with the side of my blade. Let's try again.

Taking a calming breath, Tegain slipped back into a thoughtless state, and Lyn took control of his body. Stepping out with his left leg, she took a side-facing stance and raised the two-handed sword horizontally to head height. She waited for the dark giant to make the first move.

Fully recovered, the pitch-black armored giant adjusted his grip on the battle-axe. Moving one hand farther up the haft, he placed his other near the bottom. He stepped forward with his left leg to mirror Lyn's stance.

Lyn and the Dread Lord faced off, each waiting for the other to move. She knew from watching countless master swordsmen that the first move was the first mistake. Every attack had a counter, but not every counter could be defeated. Of course, many of her wielders had dispensed with swordplay once they found that she could cut through anything. No one could defend when their weapon was cut to pieces.

Tired of waiting and with his goal before him, the Dread Lord broke the standoff. He prepared for an overhead chop despite no room to do so. As the battle-axe encountered the ceiling, it never slowed. However, Lyn could see by the position of his hands his true intention. During mid-swing, the giant changed from an overhead swing to a thrust with the butt of the handle. As he reversed the head and brought up the haft, she thrust forward between his arms.

Releasing his hold on the bottom of the haft to avoid losing his hand, he continued the attack single-handed. Lyn easily deflected the coming blow with the side of the extended blade. Reversing his swing again and returning his grip, the Dread Lord stepped in to deliver a short sideways chop. Not wanting to block with the blade, Lyn sidestepped and leaned back to allow the vicious strike to pass. However, the Dread Lord had stopped the short chop and again struck out with the haft.

Lyn backpedaled to stay out of range of the giant. She was hampered by the inability to block with the sword, which caused her to lose ground. Blow after blow rained upon her from every angle, and she gave more ground each time. Giving up ground wasn't good; she had no idea what she could be backing into. She would have to go on the offensive, even though it might mean hitting edges again.

Dropping low, Lyn performed a pirouette with the blade held extended horizontally at knee height. The giant leapt back to keep from having his leg severed. Now it was the Dread Lord on the defensive as Lyn pressed her attack. Deflecting some of her swings with the head of the battle-axe, he too seemed unwilling to cause another explosion.

They were equally skilled. However, the giant had the advantage of reach with his weapon. Lyn and the Dread Lord danced back and forth about the tunnel, neither truly gaining the upper hand for what seemed like hours to Tegain, until finally it happened. Lyn had been pushed farther back into the passage than ever by a particularly savage assault. When she made her move to counter, the edge of their weapons came in contact for the second time. They had been swinging full force at one another.

Where the weapons impacted, space seemed to distort and collapse for a moment before exploding outward in a powerful blast. The two combatants were sent flying in opposite directions. Tegain was blinded and deafened by the explosion. Hitting the ground after a short flight, he could still feel the whole mountain shaking. Tremors seemed to continue for quite some time. When he was able to see again, he understood why. A solid wall of rocks and rubble filled the area where the exit used to be. If not for being blown backwards, he would have surely been crushed.

"Well, I guess we're done with him," breathed Tegain.

Only for a little while. I can still feel his presence. So, he must still live, and if he still lives, I don't think he will stop coming after us.

"Aye, I feel you are right. What should we do now?"

As I see it, there is only one direction left open for us to go. And it just so happens to be in the direction we are wanting to go.

"So much for not disturbing the ire of whatever is down here."

I think caving in the passageway might have already done that.

"Indeed, it may have." A low thumping began to reverberate from the freshly fallen rock.

I know we are only delaying the inevitable; it may give us time to come up with a plan against this foe.

Looking back one last time at the cave-in, Tegain turned down the pitch-black passageway and descended deeper into the dark. Several tunnels intersected the main passage as he traveled, but none seemed too appealing. They were all about half the size of a man. Keeping to the central tunnel, he walked for what seemed miles.

"Am I still sped up?" he asked.

No, I released that cyne after the cave-in.

"We've been walking for hours. How long do these tunnels go on?"

Your guess is as good as mine. I never knew something like this could exist.

They continued to march quietly in the darkness, always sticking to the largest passageway. Through the twists and turns, Tegain would have been totally lost. However, the increasing sensation of the distant threat kept his sense of direction anchored to the south. He could still feel the giant knight behind him to the north, but that feeling had grown weaker and weaker with every step.

After many more hours of wandering in the darkened passageways, they came upon a wide-open grotto. Here the structure of the walls returned to a natural-looking rock. Water dripped far off in the distance. Moist, musty air filled his lungs as he took in a deep breath.

"This is different," said Tegain.

We must be miles under the surface.

With his helm giving him daylight-enhanced vision, wondrous colors danced along the huge columns that stretched from floor to the ceiling high above. Stalactites and stalagmites sprouted from random locations all along the floor and the roof of the space. It was alien and awe-inspiring all at the same time. He stopped to take in the spectacle.

"It is beautiful." His voice echoed out into the open space.

I have never seen the like in all my years, whispered Lyn in his mind.

"Without the helmet, I doubt the light of lanterns could reveal all of this."

Indeed, wondrous, just wondrous.

Starting out again, Tegain took in the splendor around him as he walked. The mammoth grotto continued for as far as he could see. Many new and marvelous sights greeted them as they trekked southward toward the growing sensation of impending doom. The feeling of the Dread Lord faded off to nothingness at some point along the journey.

*   *   *

Watching from high up among the stalactites, a solitary young vilekin queen observed the lone figure far below. Her visual spectrum was only in the infrared. To her the grotto sparkled in hues of violet, indigo and blue, the small figure shone bright white in the coolness around him. Not long ago, the entire mountain had shaken from a cave-in, and now this stranger had delved deep into her home. She had returned to the place of her birth after losing her first brood in the surface city. Wary of the intruder, she did not wish to risk discovery. Perhaps he was only passing through.

He did not look like one of the dark ones that had pushed them from their home. They had lost so many. Her kin had set these tunnels and grottos aglow, and now there was only she. Dark ones had come to the southern tunnels, and they had slaughtered anything in their path. When they could not be slowed or stopped, the old matron had fled to the surface to escape them. She had returned here after the old queen had died in the city far to the east.

With her new eggs safely tucked at the base of a massive stalactite, she followed the intruder. Keeping to the ceiling, the young queen stealthily navigated the roof of the cavern just as easily as if she were on the ground. If the stranger continued, he would soon reach the decimated tunnels.

* * *

Blown from his feet by the explosion of the two soul-forged weapons, the Dread Lord was nearly thrown out of the tunnel. Blinded and dazed, he took a moment to regain his bearings. Rising to his feet, he could now see the rubble and debris blocking the passageway. He could feel the false commander farther down the tunnel. The tang of bile filled his mouth. His eye slits flared as fury overcame him. As he slammed the battle-ax repeatedly into the rockslide, chunks of rock and debris flew with every blow.

Venting his frustration on the cave-in, the Dread Lord steadily chopped a path through the rubble. Most of the blockage was a single slab of granite that had filled the tunnel. Never tiring, he continued to chip away at the rock for hours on end. Eventually, the Dread Lord broke through the opposite end of the cave-in. It had taken over a day of constant labor. And still, he burned with fury. He could no longer feel the direction of the false commander. Nevertheless, there was only one path before him.

Proceeding down the dark passageway, the Dread Lord strode with a ground-eating pace. It was not long before he entered the subterranean cavern deep below the Hittons. Here he could feel the false commander some distance to the south. If he were to catch him unaware again, he would have to release his anger and not wish harm upon him. One of the many properties of their cyne-enhanced armor was to warn of impending threats.

After a few moments of concentration, he gave up; his hate for the little man and sword were too great. The false commander would not escape, and he would bring this sword to his master.

Let him fear my coming, concluded the Dread Lord as he continued south through the grotto.

*   *   *

Vyckie had charged to the east to find a way down to Tegain. Solar and Solis had nearly set, and she still had not found an area in the deep, narrow canyon open enough to allow her access to the bottom. She could now sense that Tegain had finally risen, but he was traveling farther away to the south.

No matter what, she would have to cross the ravine to continue south. She worked a path in the deep snow leading up to the cliff edge. Once there was sufficient runway, she made her way to the start of the cleared lane and galloped headlong toward the deep divide. Driving her powerful six legs into the edge of the cliff, she launched herself high into the air to soar over the sixty-foot gap.

Landing heavily in the deep snow on the opposite side of the canyon, Vyckie rolled head over hoof before righting herself. Without pause, she shook the impacted snow from her mane and body and set out again in Tegain's direction. Non-stop during the starlit night, she plowed through the heavy snow until she reached the spot on the opposite side of the canyon where Tegain had fallen.

Turning to the south, she made her way through deep snow over the nearest pass between the towering peaks. The way was treacherous, and many times she had to turn back and find another path. Soon Solis and Solar set once again. Deep in the cracks of the mountain, not even the light of the stars showed. Unable to see in pitch darkness, she stopped to wait out the night. Only with the suns' morning light, would she be able to continue her search.

*   *   *

Tegain had no idea how long he had spent traversing the mammoth cave when, finally, the roof and walls began to narrow. Unexpectedly, the smell of rotting flesh became almost overpowering. It was some distance before they came upon the signs of the battle. At the end of the grotto lay the remains of thousands upon thousands of vilekin of various sizes. Stalactites and stalagmites had been cut cleanly in two and were shattered about the cavern floor. It was more like a slaughter. Here and there lay the twisted remains of the metal-like beasts that had attacked him at Talenshan.

His eyes burned, and he tried to keep from gagging. "They must have tried to stop them here."

By the Nine, I have never seen such carnage in all my years. I do believe they mean to destroy us all.

"Why would anything want to do that?"

I think these things are not of Krysin. Somehow, they traveled here, and they mean to conquer our home.

"Traveled from where?"

From the multitude of other planets that must be out there. I think it safe to assume that there must be other planets near the other stars in the night sky.

"I never thought about it."

I've had plenty of time to wonder about our place in all of creation.

His armor pulsated with a sharp needle like sensation all along his spine. Tegain knew a threat was coming from behind him. "I think the dark knight made it through the cave-in."

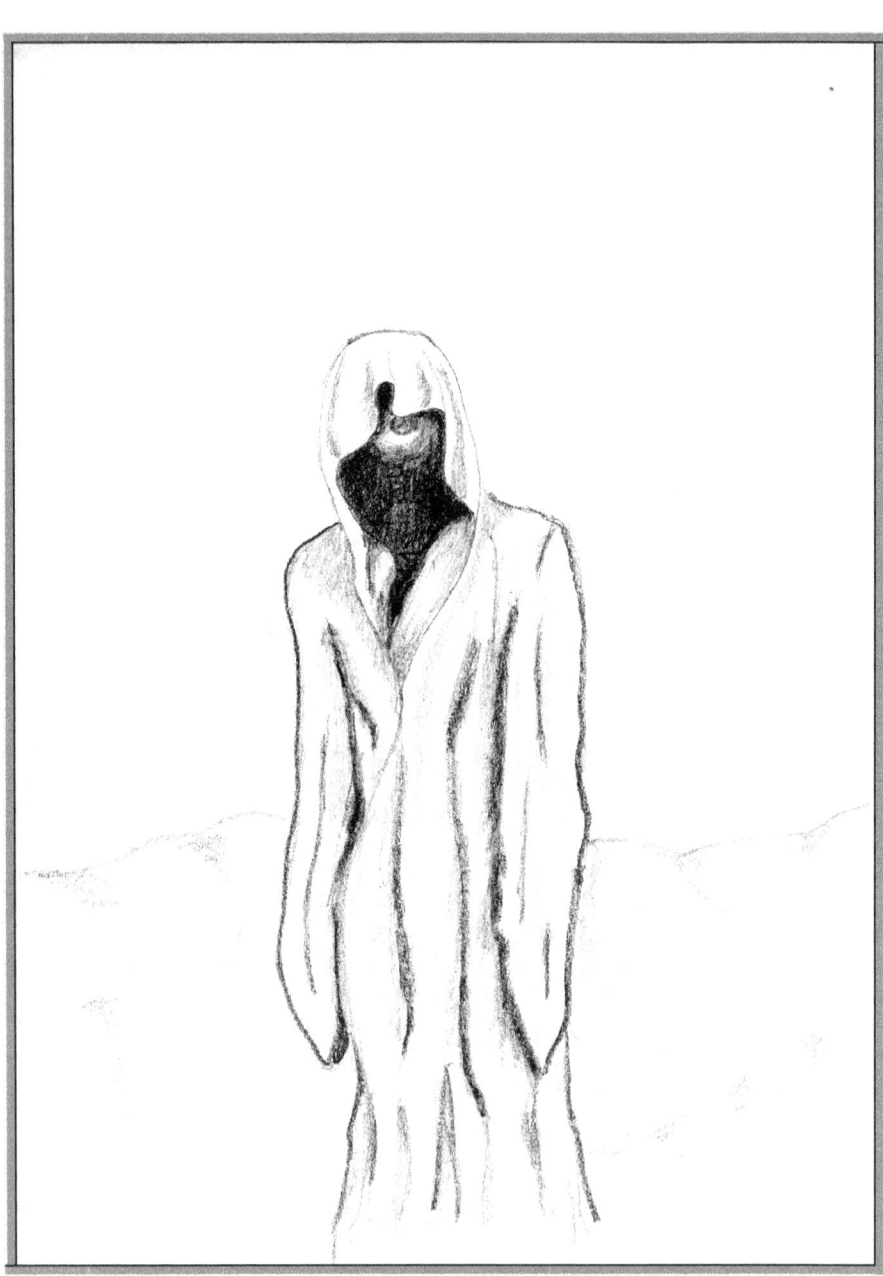

CHAPTER 10

"Retreatin' only be attackin' in the opposite direction."

-Karl Dunmire

Through the night, wagons were loaded and preparations completed for the monumental effort of evacuating Talenshan. Karl and Brent had foreseen the possibility of abandoning the city if the myders came before they were ready. Karl had hoped to use the myders' own fiery tubes against them. Alas, Master Kord had not yet figured out how to make them work.

Some of the Waymen's horses were commandeered to draw the many carts needed to haul the supplies stored around the city. This had not been a part of the original plan. Before the arrival of the Royal Wayman Dragoons, they would have left with only what they could personally carry. However, with Marshal Donaldson and his regiment of Waymen Dragoons, there were more than enough horses to transport everything needed. Those Waymen giving up their horses would be used as guards for the wagons.

Lieutenant Scott had protested at first saying, "Marshal Donaldson would not approve of the appropriation of the Waymen in such a manner."

"And where be your captain marshal, now?" retorted Karl. "I be a captain marshal. Ye be taking orders from me. If Donaldson be returning, I be taking care o' him."

Once everything was set in motion, Karl had taken a moment to clean his armor on the steps leading up to the transfigured city hall. From out of the darkness, Captain Brent approached as Karl sat polishing his armor by the light of a lantern.

"You know you could have someone do that for you?" suggested Brent.

"Aye, but I be finding it relaxing, and it be giving me time to reflect," said Karl. "Do ye be getting everything ready to go?"

"Aye, Captain Marshal, everything is going to plan, though some on the council don't feel it necessary to leave," said Brent.

"Bah, councils, I be done with councils. If they be wishing to stay, then let them be staying. But they be staying with no dragoons. Have ye be seeing Captain Marshal Donaldson?"

"No, I have not, but Captain Scott says the Waymen will be ready before suns' rise," said Brent.

"Good…" Karl trailed off, lost in thought for a moment. "I be leaving ye in charge o' protecting the folk while the rest o' us be chasing down these beasties. I know ye be wanting to go, but ye be the only man I be trusting."

"I figured you'd say something like that," Brent sighed. "I was hoping to be of more use."

Karl stopped his polishing and faced Brent with a stern look. "Be knowing this… Protecting the defenseless be no greater responsibility to a soldier. It means ye be the last line o' defense to be protecting what we be all holding dear. These men be trusting ye to be keeping their families safe, and I trust ye with that responsibility."

"Well, since you put it that way, how could I refuse? I am honored you put that much trust in me," said Brent.

"Fighting beasties be looking exciting, but I know what be most vital, and me mind be at ease with ye at me back. Thank ye, Brent." He proffered his arm in salutation. They grasped each other's forearms in a hearty shake.

"I guess I'd better get back to it then," said Brent.

"Aye, I'll be along shortly," offered Karl as they released their grip.

Returning to the finishing details of cleaning his armor, Karl reflected on the battle against the rock reavers. Combat had no time to allow for second-guessing. While he cleaned, he reviewed all he had experienced during the long day. What could he have done better? How could he have prevented his men from being injured or killed? Could he have helped Marshal Donaldson and his men? He mulled these questions over, and if he could have made better decisions, Karl made a mental note. He had learned over the centuries that these mental exercises improved his decisions during battle.

Thumping armored feet disturbed his musing. Raising his head, Karl saw Captain Marshal Donaldson in full dress armor stomping his way to him. Two Waymen lieutenants, Hargrove and Beihl, flanked him.

"May the Nine have mercy on me," Karl whispered to himself before the arrival of the stunted marshal and his men.

"What's this I hear? You have commandeered Waymen to haul carts?" asked Donaldson.

"Aye, we be leaving," Karl said flatly as he turned back to polishing his armor.

"*WE* are not going anywhere," asserted Donaldson. "I have made no order to abandon this city. I have put a stop to your idiotic order to evacuate. No one in their right mind would leave a perfectly defensible city to be massacred in the open field." Donaldson shared a confirming glance with each man at his side before he continued. "By the power invested in me by King—"

"Be holding yer tongue, little man," interrupted Karl, without ever looking up from his cleaning. "I be evoking me right to trial by combat."

"I have never heard of such a thing," said Donaldson.

Karl stopped his rubbing to look at Donaldson. "Of course ye have not. Be looking to the Wayman Codex of Law. Ye be finding it there. It be real close to that court martial ye be wanting to be using earlier."

Donaldson's eyes bulged, and his face turned red before he could continue. "I will do no such thing. Arrest this buffoon." Pointing at Karl, he sneered with glee.

Karl shook his head and rolled his eyes. "I know ye be following orders. So, I be sorry 'bout this." He calmly set down the piece of armor.

The two lieutenants stepped forward to apprehend him. "Sorry, about what?" asked Beihl on the left.

Karl shot to his feet and slammed his open palm between Beihl's eyes. The lieutenant's head rocked back, and he crumpled to the stairs in a heap. Hargrove tried to grab for his sword, but Karl knocked him unconscious with a quick blow to his temple. From the top of the steps, Donaldson began to draw his blade. Two quick strides brought Karl within arm's reach. He rammed the half-drawn weapon back into its scabbard with his left hand as he grasped

Donaldson's breastplate below his chin with his right. Being a couple of steps below Donaldson, he was now face-to-face with the diminutive man.

Drawing him close, Karl demanded, "If ye be not following the law, why should I?"

"Are you threatening a captain marshal of the Royal Wayman Dragoons?" spat out Donaldson.

"I be within me rights to kill ye on the spot for disregarding the Codex. I be not wanting to kill ye, though. I know ye be letting your pride direct your actions. Your pride be setting ye on a path of destruction. I be trying to do what be best for those we be protecting, but I need your help."

With a dubious look, Donaldson said, "I will not help a coward who abandons his men."

Karl sighed and shook his head slightly. "I know what be happening to ye in the catacomb. Ye be watching your men die, and ye be running for your life. Ye be abandoning your men, and ye be feeling guilty. Now, ye be accusing me of what ye yourself be doing. Be that so?"

Donaldson's face contorted as he tried to come to terms with what Karl said. Rage, fear, and guilt battled for control. His bottom lip quivered as he tried to speak. "I… I didn't know what to do… I…" He broke down into tears before he could say anymore.

"I see ye've never been losing men under your command."

Donaldson nodded as he tried to regain his composure.

"I know your pain. I be losing many men over the years. But ye not be changing the past. Ye only be changing how ye be now. Be not letting your guilt and pride keep ye from taking the right course. Ye be owing it to the men that be giving their lives and those that be still living. Men be counting on ye to be leading them."

"How do you do it?" asked Donaldson.

"What?"

"You have faced hordes of monsters with only ten men, and you don't lose a one. I encounter one beast, and I lose everyone to a man. How is that possible?"

"Ye be forgetting 'bout the wall. That be my order to man the wall when the reavers came. Harold Minot, Jacob Foote, Ben Carter, Greg Kern, and Kyle Bitern be dying because I made that decision."

"You know their names!" A look of astonishment painted his face.

"Aye, and I know Minot be having two wee ones and a wife, Claire. Foote be joining the Wayman like his father. Carter be taking care of his sister back in Crossroads. Kern be wanting to make his father and mother proud. And Bitern be recently married to Lillie."

"By the Nine, you truly know them." He slumped in Karl's grip. "I had no idea. I thought it all was for show."

"If ye want men to be following ye into battle, ye be needing to care for every man like yer brother."

"But how can you send men you care about to their death?"

"I never be making a man do anything I be not doing myself. I be giving me life for anyone of them and they be knowing it. Would ye be wanting to put your life at risk for someone who be not doing the same, or for a man who be not caring about ye?"

"I... I never thought of it that way," responded Donaldson. "I was told differently rising through the ranks."

"Aye, I know they be telling ye: be not getting attached to your men, because ye be needing to send them into harm's way. But they be wrong. Men be fighting for the man next to them. They be trusting each other with their lives. They be needing to trust ye like a brother. It be as simple as that."

Beihl and Hargrove were beginning to stir.

"I need ye to be a leader. These men be looking to ye for what needs to be doing. We be fighting for the same cause. Let's be not fighting each other," pleaded Karl as he released Donaldson's cuirass and offered his arm in friendship.

Donaldson's features hardened as he spoke. "There's something about you that is hard to resist." He grasped Karl's proffered arm. "You still need to convince me about why we are retreating from a perfectly defensible position."

"We be not retreating. We be only attacking in the opposite direction. The reavers be heading east to Fulsom then to Crossroads for certain. I also feel the myders be coming soon, and we be not ready for them. Be trusting me when I say we're not wanting to meet them if we be not having to."

"I see," said Donaldson. He absently tapped his chin with his forefinger. "It is true. I have let my pride guide my decisions as of late. There is much that needs to be corrected."

Beihl and Hargrove struggled to their feet behind Karl. Stumbling toward him from either side, both men used the old marshal more for support than to restrain him.

"That won't be necessary, gentlemen," declared Donaldson. "There was a misunderstanding, and I have been enlightened about the situation. Marshal Dunmire has been excused of any wrongdoing." Donaldson spun around and stomped off into the city hall.

"That's it?" asked Beihl after Donaldson disappeared into the catacomb.

"I feel like I got kicked by a mule," groaned Hargrove.

"I be sorry 'bout that."

Beihl took a knee. "I wish he would have just talked to you first."

"Aye, but we be running out of time. This be not the time to play games." He helped the two lieutenants recover and then make their way into the transformed city hall.

Dawn came with the yellow glow of Solar breaking above the Hittons in the west followed shortly by Solis's fiery orange. Solis would soon eclipse Solar. Krysin's winter quickly approached. Everything would take on the orange hue of Solis as the days grew colder.

As Karl sat atop Rowdy in the city square, he watched the rising suns and hoped for a mild winter. However, he knew there had been three mild winters in a row. The fourth winter was always longer and colder than the others. If they were to survive the coming cold, they needed to prevent the reavers from ransacking Crossroads. Food was already becoming scarce as many of the farmers had been unable to harvest their crops because of the attacking hordes.

With Captain Marshal Donaldson now working with Karl, the Dragoon brigade was almost fully assembled in Talenshan's city center. Five hundred or so waymen had been reassigned to protect the populace that would follow behind. Every working cart and wagon was laden with supplies or those too weak to walk.

Karl nodded to Marshal Donaldson to indicate that all was ready. Donaldson raised his hand above his head to signal the call to march. In the silence before the call, a voice rang out. Before, Marshal Donaldson relayed his command to march; he lowered his hand. All eyes turned to the disheveled man running and yelling at the far end of the square.

"Marshal Dunmire! Marshal Dunmire! I've done it," shouted Kord from the opposite end of the square. "I've done it!" He wove his way toward Karl at the south of the square, yelling the whole way. Kord arrived out of breath.

"I take it ye be getting a myder tube to work?" said Karl.

Kord took a few more moments to catch his breath before he could reply, "Yes, yes… while we were loading the wagon, suddenly something burned a hole clean through the bottom of the cart and the stones below. I've never seen anything like it!"

"Do it be still working?"

"Uh, no… But only because the heart stopped working, I think."

"That be good news, Kard, but we need to leave now. When ye be knowing why that one be different, then I think we'll be able to use it against the myder."

"Yes, yes, of course," mumbled Kord, staring at the ground in concentration. "I'll get right on it."

"Aye, ye be doing good, Kard. Thank ye."

"It's Kord," corrected the watchmaker more to himself than to anyone else.

Donaldson was staring at Karl with a questioning look. Karl shrugged and turned up his palms in response. He signaled again that all was ready to proceed. Donaldson shook his head slightly and raised his hand above his head again. When he lowered his arm, a bugle sounded the call to march. At a canter, Donaldson with Karl at his side led the procession of Dragoons out of the Talenshan city square and east toward Folsum. Two by two, the Dragoons fell in behind them in a double column file.

*   *   *

Captain Brent remained behind to organize the civilian egress from Talenshan. With the multitude of demands, he had not been able to see Karl and the men from Folsum off. He was quickly learning that getting everyone and everything ready to go was worse than chasing chickens around the yard. Finally, by late afternoon, when Solar and Solis were dipping low on the horizon, all seemed to be in order.

A motley array of carts, wagons, and people filled the city square. Brent had completed his final inspection and was standing next to Harold Bennett. He conferred with Master Bennett, who would lead the wagon train.

"I believe everything is in order," said Brent. "Let's get this rabble headed east."

"I thought I would never leave this place, especially in this manner," said Bennett through his permanent frown.

"I know exactly how you feel," said Brent. "I never dreamed I would have had to abandon Folsum, but here I am. Now, we have to leave Talenshan. I trust Marshal Dunmire. Karl always seems to know what to do."

"Aye, he does, doesn't he?" remarked Master Bennett.

"We will have to keep travelling through the night to keep pace with the waymen," said Brent.

"Aye, I had assumed as much," said Bennett. "I am surprised we've made this much progress as it stands. I would imagine it is much like herding cats."

"Ha! I thought it more like chickens, but herding cats does sound as arduous," agreed Brent.

"Indeed, may the Nine be with you," said Harold as he clucked to the team of horse pulling his wagon.

"Aye, and to you as well," called Brent as Master Bennett made his way out of the square.

To help expedite the departure, Captain Brent directed traffic leaving the city square. Slowly but surely, the city center began to empty. By the time the last cart left to the east, the darkened hues of dusk were coalescing in the square. Brent and two waymen guards stood in the shadows of the nearby buildings.

"By the Nine, that took longer than it should have," said Brent.

"Now, we have to keep them moving," said the older soldier.

"Why do you say that?"

"Some folk still don't know why we are leaving, and some still don't want to leave," replied the old wayman.

"But we announced to everyone why we were leaving," said Brent.

"Did you tell everyone personally?" asked the old soldier.

"Well, no. That would take too long. We sent messengers."

"Sending a messenger is like starting a rumor, and I think you know how a rumor can change once it gets going," said the seasoned wayman.

Brent sighed. "It looks as though I've got a lot of talking to do."

"Aye, better you than me," said the old soldier, smiling.

"Thank you…" Brent proffered his arm in greeting and paused, hoping to catch the soldier's name.

"Luke… Sergeant Luke," offered the soldier as he shook forearms with Captain Brent.

"Thank you, Sergeant Luke," said Brent. Retrieving his dark bay horse,

Brent mounted and set out to begin the task of informing everyone personally. Sergeant Luke and the other wayman took up their positions behind the line of refugees that snaked out over the plain and into the forest in the distant east.

* * *

High on the slopes of the Hittons overlooking Talenshan, the fiery glow of Solis flashed off the lenses of a solitary myder. Scout-001A watched the procession of indigenous lifeforms fleeing toward the setting suns. He had been ordered back from farther afield to observe this fortified structure. Somehow an entire wave of five thousand attack drones had been decimated near the western side of the fortification.

Over the past forty-five cycles, he had not observed anything that could have caused the loss. As he had reported in all earlier interactions, the indigenous populace possessed only archaic knowledge. Central Command advised caution and that they must control some powerful unknown technology.

Confirming the warning, he had seen the broken parts of attack drones piled into three conveyances leaving the fortification earlier. He would have to keep his distance until the next wave of ten thousand drones was ready. Then he could observe and report on this technology. Replacing the heavy brown hood over his head, Scout-001A stood erect on his carbon nanotube limbs, mimicking the native bipedal mammals.

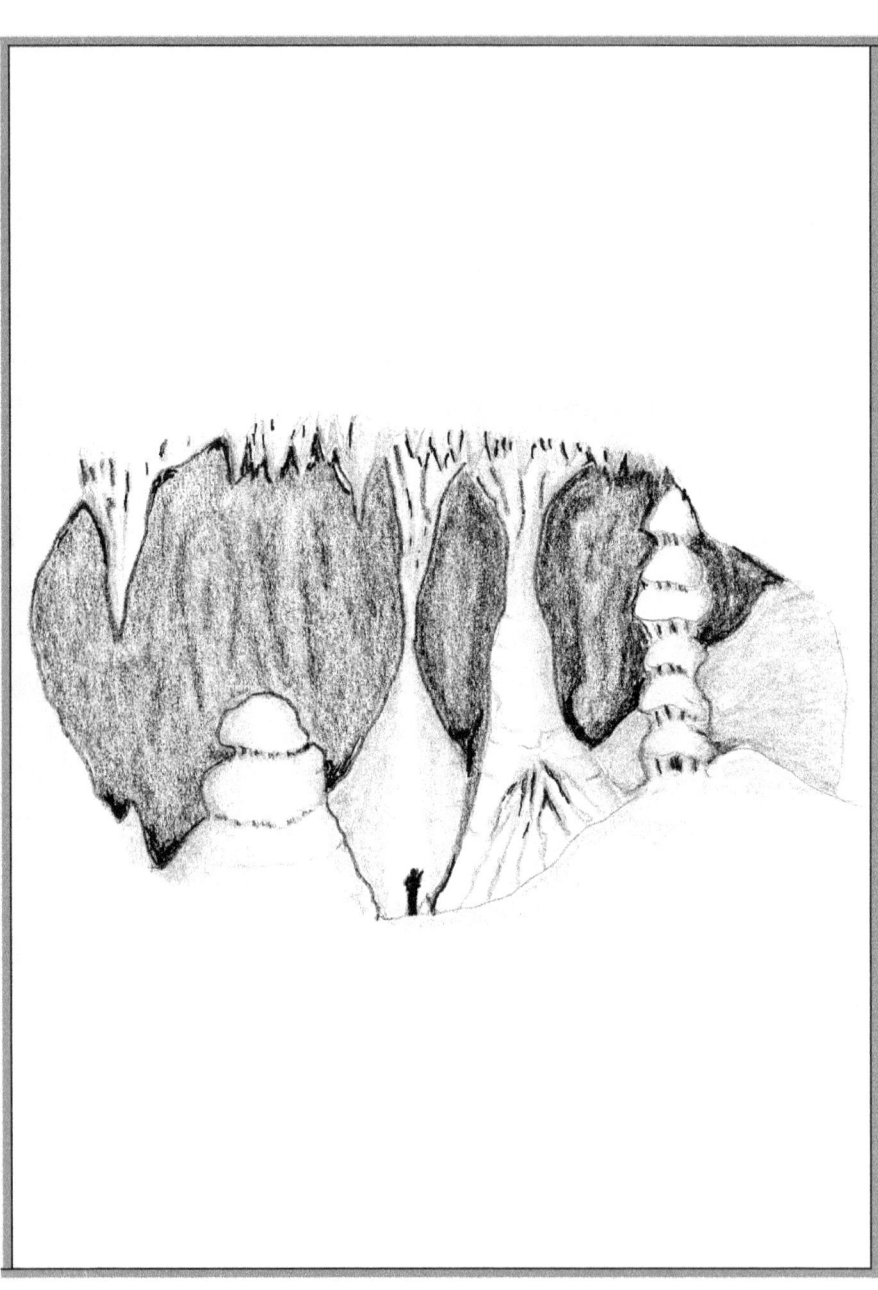

CHAPTER 11

"Answers… they only lead to more questions. I finally realized that there is no ultimate answer to end all questions. And one must be content with many questions unanswered."

-Tegain Hostler

Standing before the sea of carnage, Tegain gulped air in short shallow breaths to keep from smelling the putrescence that hung in the air. Through his stinging eyes, he could make out a black and yellowish fungus covering the carcasses piled several layers thick upon the cavern floor. Sensing the giant obsidian knight drawing closer, he knew he needed to continue forward to avoid another conflict. Carefully, he made his way over the blasted bodies and debris. Eventually, he slipped on the slick ooze of rotting flesh. After several more tumbles, he was completely covered from head to toe in putrid ichor.

"I hope this will wash off," groaned Tegain as he inspected his black, goo-covered body. "This has to be the foulest smelling stuff ever."

I couldn't agree with you more. I just hope we can find some water, and soon.

Progress was exceedingly slow, and there seemed to be no end to the massacre. Hours of slogging through decimated corpses took a mental toll on Tegain. Everywhere he stepped, touched, or looked, he saw the dead vilekin. Their husks lay shattered like pottery pitched to the floor. Trying to fathom the sheer number of bodies numbed his mind.

They must have known they were going to die, thought Tegain.

Yes… They were allowing the queen to escape.

Queen?

Yes, their queen controls the vilekin much like a hive of bees.

I see. So, they didn't really have a choice.

Yes and no. Without the queen, the vilekin are lost with no way to reproduce. I think she may also have a mental link to all her brood. I remember my father defeating just such a queen of the vilekin, and the horde seemed to lose all coordination.

Hmm, yes… I could see how losing a mental connection could be very disorienting, thought Tegain.

Would you miss me?

I can't imagine being without you now.

Ahh, you know how to touch a woman's heart.

It is true. I have never known anyone as intimately as I know you. I can sense you with me. It's hard to describe, but I would definitely notice your loss if you were gone.

I know how you feel. I can't imagine being without you. You are unlike anyone I have ever known. I think you are such a part of me that I don't know where you end and I begin.

I feel the same. He noticed he had paused his march as they conversed.

The unmistakable sensation of being watched washed over him. Tegain peered over his shoulder to the expanse behind him. There, far off in the distance, strode the giant knight. His eye slits flashed an angry red as if he knew he had been seen.

"He is already here," said Tegain.

Be at peace; it took us hours to get here. We will have time before will need to contend with him. Let's find a more suitable ground to fight upon.

His heart racing, Tegain tried to set a faster pace to the south. However, he seemed to be slipping and falling more than making forward progress. Breathing in short gasps to keep from smelling the stench, he slowly slogged his way through the massacred bodies. After what felt like an eternity, the cavern narrowed into a single path once again. In the confines of the smaller passageway, the crush of bodies ceased, and the corridor floor resumed its rough rocky texture.

Looking back over the sea of bodies, Tegain saw the giant black knight striding through the mutilated masses as if he were walking through an open field. Barely slowing to toss aside the larger carcasses that impeded his way, the obsidian goliath made steady progress toward him.

What now?

Let's see what we can do from here. Let me at him.

Tegain levelled Lyn at the distant figure. Blazing white energy began to build along her surface. As it grew, small arcs of lightning flared up and down the glaive, and she crackled like a tiny thunderstorm. With a flash, the power was released in a blinding bolt that shot out over the sea of carnage.

*   *   *

Illumination filled the cavern, and the young vilekin queen shielded her eyes from its intensity. A streaking bolt of white-hot flash burst from the tiny alcove where the stranger stood. It arced out across the shattered grotto to strike the colossal figure. Within the growing globe of light, the pitch-black outline of the giant remained unchanged. Power crackled and roared about him as he began to glow. In an instant, darkness returned and a thunderous boom shook the cavern. From the cover of her stalactite, the vilekin queen held on tightly until the tremors subsided. She peered from her distant vantage to where the orange, fiery giant stood. Even the ground around him had turned into a molten pool of rock.

As the glowing figure sank into the melted stone, his outstretched arms convulsed, and his head snapped back in a silent scream. He struggled to step free of the pool, which only succeeded in entrapping him deeper in the rapidly cooling cavern floor.

With this frightening display of power, the young vilekin queen now knew that these two intruders had caused the earlier cave-in. Why were they here? Why did they fight each other? Where were they going? These questions troubled her as she glanced back toward the distant stalactite where her eggs clung in the darkness. If the fire-spitting cold ones returned, her brood would not be safe. In her frantic flight from the surface, she had fled to the only place she knew well. The cold ones appeared to have abandoned the cavern, but with this recent activity they were sure to return.

The slim covered figure turned to continue deeper into the tunnels. By now, the larger intruder was held fast by the cooled stone. He had managed to free one leg. However, the other limb was encased well above the knee joint. Lying on his back, the cooling giant appeared to have succumbed to his wounds. From her high vantage, the young vilekin queen saw the goliath's eyes come ablaze as he came back to life. Perhaps, he too was as strong as the little slimy creature.

An idea came to her. If she could lead these powerful strangers to the cold ones, perhaps they could rid her home of them. A small smile pulled at the corners of her alabaster lips. If they were unsuccessful, then she would look for a new home. However, if they succeeded in destroying the cold ones, she could return home in peace. With amazing alacrity, she sped along the ceiling. In mere seconds, she disappeared into a secondary passageway that would take her ahead of the shiny creature.

*   *   *

As he traversed the putrid grotto, a flash of white light filled the Dread Lord's vision, and then the pain began. His armor shielded him from the electrical force of the attack, but it had been unable to keep from dissipating the tremendous amount of heat. While he sank into the molten floor, he could feel his flesh turning to ash as quickly as it was restored. With his nerve endings endlessly regenerating, the excruciating pain only intensified with every second. His involuntary reaction had been to scream. If he had possessed a voice, his wail would have rivaled that of the blast delivered from the little man's sword. Before he could free himself from the cooling rock, the Dread Lord had succumbed to the pain.

When he finally awoke, he was lying on his back with his armor still cooling and his right leg held fast in the cave floor. His mind still reeling with pain, he struggled to rise. After a few heroic attempts to stand, he resorted to a semi-squatting position with his hands on the ground for support, while his trapped leg remained buried midway up his thigh. The Dread Lord pounded the ground in frustration. Pulverized rock sprayed out from under his armored fist. Pummeling the freshly cooled stone to free his leg crossed his mind; he dismissed the notion after considering how long it would take. More than anything, he wanted to crush this false commander. Every second of delay would carry the little man farther away.

Unlimbering his two-handed battle-axe, the obsidian giant steeled himself for what he must do. His awkward position did not allow him to put much force behind his swing. Nevertheless, the soul-enhanced weapon easily cleaved through his encased leg. With fresh pain came freedom. Using the enlarged battle-axe, the Dread Lord levered himself up onto his remaining leg. His armor tightened around his severed limb to keep him from bleeding to death. Leaning heavily on the haft of his weapon to fight back a wash of pain, the giant took several moments to recover. Once the spasm had subsided, he began the task of cutting out the stone surrounding his trapped leg.

Laboring without the use of both legs, the Dread Lord struggled to maintain his footing between swings. After several hours, he had hewn out a sunken pillar containing his severed limb. Satisfied that enough material had been removed, he lowered himself down onto the entombed leg. Agony assailed him as his limb began to return to life. The torment of a thousand cuts coursed through him as feeling slowly crept down his lifeless limb. Cold blood began to push its way back into his body. His chest tightened, and his left arm went numb when the thick clot of cold blood slammed into his heart.

After a time, his suffering abated, and he felt the use of his once-severed appendage nearly restored. He tried freeing his leg with a few upward jerks. However, the hardened stone held tightly to its prize. Raising his massive battle-axe above his head, he brought the side of the double-bladed weapon down against it. Sparks and a spray of crushed stone flew as the soul-forged weapon slammed into the side of the pillar. The metal axe head rang out with a high-pitched peal that filled the grotto.

Spidery fissures snaked out from the point of impact to cover the side of the stone encasement. He could feel the pressure lessen slightly around his pinned limb. As he shifted his weight to push against the weakened side, the pillar groaned under the strain. With a resounding crack, the damaged encasement crumbled to pieces, and the Dread Lord stepped free of the stony trap. Venting his frustration, he crushed what remained of the pillar with several powerful stomps from his armored foot. With his anger sated, the obsidian giant leaped from the hole and began anew his task of hunting down the false commander.

*　　*　　*

Night and day, Vyckie trekked without pause over high mountain passes and through snow-filled valleys in an effort to keep pace with Tegain. She could feel him deep underground and ever moving southward. Many times, she had to backtrack and take a circuitous route when his path went where she could not go. Nothing would deter her from staying as close to him as possible. When he returned to the surface, she would be there waiting for him.

Heavy clouds had begun to gather since morning, and soon they would unleash their wintery fury upon the monumental peaks. This time, Vyckie had no place to go to escape the onslaught that embattled the shallow ravine where she had stopped. Crisp, still air from this morning now howled like an enraged beast, and her frosty breath was torn from her muzzle with each fresh blast that ripped down from high in the mountains.

Wind-blown snow stung at her face, despite her turning her back toward the brunt of the tempest, and she was forced to keep her head low with her eyes squeezed shut. While she remained as still as possible, drifts of snow eventually covered her entire body. By tucking her head close to her chest, she was able to maintain a small space in which to breathe. With a few long, shallow breaths, Vyckie slowed down her metabolism until her heart only beat once every hour, and her respiration diminished to the same.

But this time, in her state of suspended animation, she left her hearing fully functional. When the wailing gale abated, she would know she could continue her journey. Time faded, and only the sound of the tempest floated in her thoughts. Buried under an ever-increasing amount of snow, she patiently waited for silence.

*　　*　　*

After the reverberations from the blast subsided, Tegain watched in awe as the giant, glowing knight struggled to escape the newly formed molten pool of stone. "How did he survive that?" he said under his breath.

I can only assume his armor shielded him in some way.

"What now?" wondered Tegain.

That is a very good question—one I don't have an answer for yet. He is definitely very tenacious.

"I would have to agree." Watching the struggling giant, he felt great pity for him. "I wish we didn't have to hurt him. I have a feeling he didn't have much of a choice in the matter. Why would this Hael Atos send this man after me? Why would he even care?"

Recalling what her father had told her of Hael Atos, Lyn shared her tale. *From what I can remember, Hael was once a solitary shepherd. During countless lonely hours tending his flock, he discovered the ability to cyne. Yes, Hael Atos was the first cynosure. Though, during that time, they were not called so. Many thought him a wizard or sorcerer and were frightened by what he could do. Hael insisted that anyone could learn to do the same as he if they took the time. He envisioned a place where everyone could create whatever they desired. There would no longer be any lack, and no one would wish to rule over anyone. Everyone would truly be free.*

To prove it, he would teach anyone who wished to learn. Hael created a simple school situated near the southern Hittons, open to anyone who wished to learn. As word and excitement spread, many people came. Even the king at the time sent one of his daughters to Hael's school. Most gave up after a short while when they found how much time and discipline it required—as you know, from your experience making your first cyne. Can you imagine sitting in concentration without the benefit of your armor? Hael, however, was extremely adept at cyning. He could create a cyne almost instantly and with exquisite detail. From either his hours of training, luck, or both, Hael's mind seemed to visualize with little effort. Without a doubt, he was the first Master.

After a few months, only nine had stayed from the multitudes that had flocked to the school. The remaining followers began calling themselves cynosures. One of them was my father. For months, my father and the other cynosures trained their minds. Progress was extremely slow. With so many quitting and those who stayed unable to cyne after nearly a year, folks began to think that Hael could not teach cyning to others.

One day, the king came to see what his daughter had learned after so much study. When she failed to produce a cyne, he became upset. She tried to explain that she was nervous and couldn't concentrate, but the king would not have any of it. Hael was brought before him to explain why his daughter, after so long, could still not cyne.

Standing before the king, Hael admitted that it had taken him nearly ten years to perfect his ability and that, judging by the progress so far, it would take much longer for most to learn how to cyne. Hael thought perhaps her youthful mind might learn more quickly, but he did not know for sure. It seemed that everyone else learned to cyne at a much slower pace than he had.

From what my father told me, the king left that day seemingly satisfied by Hael's answer. However, sometime later, a legion of the king's soldiers marched into the school. They proclaimed the school closed and took everyone into custody. No reason was given, but I think that perhaps the king feared that Hael and those he taught to cyne would usurp his rule.

They were all brought to the king's palace in the capital city of Huron. During the long journey, they were continually tortured and knocked unconscious to keep them from cyning. My father did not speak much of what happened to them, but I remember him saying that what they had done to Hael was unspeakable.

My father believed the king had planned to make an example of Hael and those who could cyne. He was unconscious at the time, but my father was told that as they neared the gates of the capital, Hael awoke and cried out moments before he vanished in a beam of light that came from the sky.

Shortly thereafter, men in the legion marching them to the city began to die. One by one, each soldier suffered an excruciatingly painful demise. A powerful invisible force slowly crushed and tore them limb from limb. Some tried to run or defend themselves. Others cried and pleaded for mercy. They were shown none.

When the cries of the last dying man faded, Hael appeared to the cynosures and communicated directly to their minds. I am not sure what Hael told them, but from then on, they were on their own. Hael forsook humanity that day. He turned from his disciples and disappeared along with the entire capital city of Huron. All that remained of the once great city was a huge crater, as if it had been scooped up by a giant hand.

I think Hael cares not for the struggles of mankind. In fact, from what I can remember, he delighted in our suffering.

Surely, he can't still be alive, thought Tegain.

He is a Master. I don't think it unreasonable that he could still be alive.

No, I mean the giant.

Oh, about him, I'm not certain, but it does appear he is stuck in the floor of the cavern.

Yes, I can kind of understand why Hael would send this man, but how could someone hold a grudge that long?

I know from experience that too much time has a way of twisting your mind.

Are you suggesting that you're not right in the head? A small smile pursed his lips.

Ha! I haven't had a head to be "right in" for so long I'm not sure.

Ah, yes there is that. Hopefully, we can do something about that soon. I will return you to your body.

Oh, you have no idea how wonderful that makes me feel; but first there is this small issue of impending eradication, said Lyn.

From an ancient lunatic or metallic spiders?

Take your pick.

"I think our giant friend may be stuck for a while, and I don't wish to wade out into that mess again," said Tegain. "I guess that leaves me with alien spiders, though I could really use a bath before that."

Yes… yes, you definitely do need a bath.

Sighing heavily, Tegain turned from the decimated grotto and retreated deeper into the smaller tunnel.

In the darkness behind him, he could faintly hear something skittering stealthily into another passage. Little time passed before Tegain again could feel the presence of the goliath.

CHAPTER 12

"Talkin' never be gettin' anything done."

-Karl Dunmire

After a full day of marching, the nearly unmolested city of Folsum came into view. Karl's grueling pace had not allowed for a break the entire day. In the dim orange light of the dual setting suns, the hard outlines of the buildings stood out starkly. Reaching the town limits, Captain Marshal Donaldson called for the columns to halt.

"We should stop here for the night," he said, looking to Karl for confirmation.

"Are ye thinking the beasties be thinking the same?"

Marshal Donaldson frowned heavily before he replied, "No, but I don't want to push the men to exhaustion right before a battle."

"I don't think the rock reavers be caring if we be tired or not."

"Aye, I know you are right, but I don't think I want to continue much longer," admitted Donaldson. "I am too weary from the day's ride, and we would need lights to continue on in the dark. Those might draw unwanted attention."

"Aye," said Karl, and he spent some time in self-reflection. "All right, let's be setting up a cold camp. No more than a few hours rest." With that, Donaldson immediately gave the order to dismount and prepare a fireless camp.

In the deepening darkness, the both columns of men dismounted and preparation for a dark camp was carried out. Solar and Solis set as tandem balls of fire. The orange hue of Solis lingered as a reminder of the colder days to come. Karl ensured that Rowdy was taken care of, and then he made a simple bed from his pad and saddle. Once the last light of the suns vanished, the clamor of camp noise diminished to a dull din that lulled him to a fitful rest.

As Karl dreamed, visions of the past melded into the urgent needs of the present. Battles against bandits and vilekin warped into endless melees that had no victor. He struggled in the dream to bring each combatant to yield under his expert swordsmanship, but before he could make the decisive maneuver, they seemed to slip away.

"Marshal Dunmire… Marshal Dunmire, it is time to wake," Jarid's voice echoed over his fitful dream of a towering grimble.

Karl's eyes snapped open as he came awake, and before he could regain his senses, he had levelled his dagger inches from Jarid's eye.

Realizing where he was, Karl halted his thrust and lowered his weapon. Breathing a sigh of relief, he said, "By the Nine, ye be getting too close to me, boy. I be thinking ye be a grimble."

"I'm sorry, Marshal Dunmire," gulped Jarid as he jumped to his feet.

"Mayhap, ye be using a stick next time ye wake me."

"Uh, aye, Marshal, I will," said Jarid in a trembling voice. "It is the hour before suns' rise as you requested."

"Aye, thank ye, Jarid."

With shaking hands, Jarid picked up the small lantern sitting on the ground. Lowering the hood to allow only a tiny circle of light, he hurriedly set out to complete his rounds.

"I be getting too old for this," Karl whispered to himself. "Me dreams be getting to me." Taking a moment to rub his hands over his bald head, he breathed in deeply and let it out in a long, slow release. With that, he began his morning ritual of calisthenics. He needed to clear his mind before the start of the day. As he worked his body, he focused his mind on the physical activity. In a short time, everything around him faded, and all that existed was motion and exertion.

Karl tried beginning every day with an exercise routine. On those days that he couldn't, things seemed not to go as smoothly. For him, the physical exercise focused his mind the same as meditation did for cynosures. Somehow, through his rigorous routine, he had acquired some powers of the cynosures. Years of this type of meditation had given him extended life and the ability to sometimes cyne.

Yellow-orange hues illuminated the distant peaks of the Hittons as Karl finished his routine. Somewhere along the column of slumbering men, a bugle signaled the call to awaken and prepare for the day's march. Three quick, sharp notes followed by a single long note completed the call to "roust and ride." Feeling relaxed and invigorated, Karl stowed his gear and readied Rowdy while he sucked on a hardened piece of bread called a stone biscuit. Before he had completed his preparations, Captain Marshal Donaldson arrived atop his black mare.

"It appears you slept about as well as I," commented Donaldson.

Karl glanced up from tying off his cinch to notice Donaldson's bloodshot eyes. "Aye, I be spending more time fighting me dreams than sleeping, that be for certain." He continued saddling Rowdy. Finished with the tack, he strapped his bedroll in place behind the saddle and mounted in one smooth motion.

"How do you do it?" asked Donaldson.

"What be that?"

"You move like a man half your age," said the younger captain marshal.

"Hmm… I think any man half me age be not moving much at all," Karl said with a laugh.

"Ah, yes that's right. I forget you are as old as you say…" Donaldson trailed off with an expectant look on his face, clearly hoping Karl would give some sort of hint.

"I be forgetting, too," said Karl with a dismissive shrug. He had heard the whispers of a growing sum of coppers among the soldiers betting on his exact age. Almost everyone had a guess, but the real challenge had been in trying to find out Karl's actual age, and he expertly dodged every attempt at acquiring it. Donaldson now appeared to have thrown his coppers into the pot.

Karl smiled briefly to himself. He knew exactly how old he was, and he wasn't about to divulge that information without first having a little fun. Perhaps, if the amount rose high enough, he would be tempted to end the escapade. In the meantime, the distraction boosted morale and kept their minds off the drudgery of marching.

"Do ye be hearing from the scouts?" said Karl.

"Nay, not yet. I thought maybe the reavers got about half a day on us," replied Donaldson as they set out through the streets of Fulsom. "I would think they should be showing up soon."

Karl frowned as he considered how much time had passed since sending out the first scouts. Even with half a day's head start, one pair of the six scouts should have made it back by now. "Aye, I be thinking the same," he voiced. "I be wondering what else be coming out o' the bowels o' the Hittons. There be far worse than reavers, vilekin, and grimble buried in history. By the Nine, I hope Tegain be up to the task."

"Did you say Tegain, the innkeep of the Hooded Lantern?" asked Donaldson.

"Aye, he be the one. Excepting he be no innkeep now."

"Is that so? What task are you hoping he is up to?"

"Saving us from the myders," Karl gave a worried glance back to the west.

"Ha! Surely you jest?" scoffed the miniature marshal. "From what I heard tell, he was quite a rotund fellow. I can't imagine he would be saving much of anything but a hardy meal."

Karl raised an eyebrow as he looked askance at Donaldson. "I think ye'd not be saying that, if ye be seeing what I did at Talenshan."

"Ah, yes, the great battle at the gates of Talenshan," mocked Donaldson. "I find it hard to believe such preposterous tales. Lightning bolts from a sword, no less. Extraordinary events require extra ordinary proof. "

"Are the wrecked bodies of thousands of myders not proof enough?"

"They could have been dispatched by those vilekin that had overrun the city before your arrival," explained Donaldson. "And you showed the vilekin the might of the Royal Wayman Dragoons. I think these myders are the least of our worries."

Karl furrowed his brow as he considered whether it was worth attempting to persuade the   marshal otherwise. "Ye and I be of different minds on that point, but the reavers be a more pressing issue at the moment."

As they reached the center of Fulsom, the clatter from the column of horses in the empty square ceased further conversation. Donaldson nodded his head and seemed pleased with himself.

Karl's gut sank as he realized that Donaldson truly believed the waymen could defeat the myders. Shaking his head and sighing heavily, he decided to fight that battle when the time came. They rode in silence the rest of the way through Fulsom's abandoned streets.

Solar and Solis had topped the Hittons, and Fulsom had passed from view when finally an arrow trailing a green ribbon pierced the sky far in the east. Both Donaldson and Karl breathed a sigh of relief. It signaled the return of one of the forward observers.

"I be thinking the worst," said Karl.

"I had my doubts as well," agreed Donaldson.

Quickening their pace, they hastened to meet the approaching scout. The Trader Way wound through the thick-forested hills, preventing them from seeing more than the next bend in the road. After several turns, the dust trail from a galloping horse was visible above the trees. Rounding a jutting turn devoid of foliage, they caught a fleeting glimpse of a rider at a full gallop on the opposite ridge-line, with a deep ravine spanning the distance between them.

Forced to take the circuitous route carved by the Way, they plunged back onto the thick tree-lined path. Within the confines of the forested roadway, the noise of the double column of cantering horses dampened to a degree, and heavy shadows enveloped them in a premature dusk.

Noticing that their pace had increased to nearly a gallop, Karl called out over the din to Donaldson, "Be holding up, Captain Marshal. We be not wanting to be smacking into him."

Karl's words seemed to jolt Donaldson out of a trance. He took a moment to register what Karl said. "Yes, yes of course," he mumbled, as he raised his closed fist to signal a halt. Waiting a few moments for the command to reach the back of the column, he brought his fist down and leaned back in his saddle to slow his black mare. In perfect unison, the double column of two thousand horses came to an abrupt stop.

Karl felt pleased that the Dragoons could still take the clamoring of thousands of horses and turn it to near silence with a drop of a fist. From the fresh quiet, the sound of a galloping horse echoed softly in the dense forest. In moments, a rider appeared from around the bend. Behind him trailed a riderless horse. Donaldson and Karl shared a look. They knew the rider was Liam, the forward observer sent out this morning.

"By the Nine," breathed Karl. "I be speaking too soon."

"By the Nine," repeated Donaldson from under his breath.

Sliding to a stop on his grey gelding, Liam saluted with his right fist to his chest. Karl and Donaldson returned the salute.

"Captain Marshal, permission to report," said Liam once he caught his breath.

"Permission granted," Donaldson and Karl said in unison. Donaldson looked askance at Karl.

Shrugging, Karl smirked as he explained, "Old habits be hard to let go."

"Hmm," grunted Donaldson. He looked back to Liam and nodded for him to continue.

"Sir, I found this horse wandering down the road. I think it's one of ours," reported Liam.

"We don't know for sure. It could be some farmer's stock," said Donaldson.

"Aye, it be one of ours," confirmed Karl.

"Is that so?" said Donaldson.

"Aye, it be Derrick's mount."

"How do you know?"

"It be having a snip, star, and a white fetlock on the back right hoof. That be Derrick's mare."

"Don't tell me you know all of our men's horses, too?" demanded

Donaldson, a look of incredulity plastered on his face.

"Ha, that be a trick, be it not? But no, I only be knowing the horse o' men we be sending out scouting. It sometimes be good to know."

"Hmm, indeed," agreed Donaldson reluctantly. "But this doesn't give us any information about what caused this."

"I have a feeling we be finding Derrick and Timothy's camp somewhere up the Way. Mayhap, then we be finding out more."

Donaldson took a moment to consider the situation before he spoke. "I guess we don't have much of a choice. Liam, take us to where you found Derrick's horse, and we will start our search from there."

"Aye, Captain Marshal," said Liam with a quick salute.

Once Derrick's mare was taken to the rear, they set out again with Liam taking the lead. Over an hour passed before he finally signaled for a halt.

"This is it," he announced.

During their trek, they had passed out of the steep hills. Karl noticed that they were near where Tegain and he had encountered the first grimbles. A pang of sadness pulled at his heart as he remembered Gina. She had been slaughtered by grimbles shortly after finding Tegain at his destroyed inn. They had shared the road for nearly all her life. She had pulled him and their little cart all over Tulane. He would always have fond memories of his little Gina and the time they had spent together.

"Hmm, I don't see much of anything here," said Donaldson.

"Aye, she be following the way back after she be escaping from whatever got our men. We be having to go look for them."

"We don't have time to spend searching for scouts; even this has delayed us. We need to be moving," said Donaldson.

"Let me be taking a few men to find their camp, and the rest of ye be continuing after the reavers."

Donaldson frowned and rubbed his chin while he considered. "How many men?"

"I be thinking one hundred be enough."

"A hundred! You can have thirty and no more."

In an effort to keep from smiling, Karl tried to turn the corners of his mouth down to look displeased. He had needed at least ten men, so he had asked for ten times what he required in the hopes of getting at least that many. He had learned long ago that if he asked for something, he was sure to receive less, especially when dealing with the military. For some reason, when he asked for absurdly high or low numbers, most folks had a hard time letting go of the number, and he almost always ended up making a great deal of profit.

Struggling mightily to seem disappointed, Karl conceded, "Thirty it be then."

Karl called back down the double line of men, "I be needing thirty men. Who be with me?" Every man within earshot began breaking ranks to form up behind Karl. Men and horse pushed and shoved each other in an effort to get there first.

"By the Nine, I don't know how you do it," breathed Donaldson. "They're literally fighting to follow you."

"I think they be tired of marching and be wanting to do something different."

"Perhaps," mused Donaldson. "Perhaps."

"I'll be catching up as soon as we finish here."

Donaldson signaled to move forward again. As the column of horses started out, Karl set to the task of organizing his thirty volunteers. Indeed, he had to settle some disputes as to who got there first. When all was in order, Donaldson and the rest of the Dragoons had nearly passed from view. Of course, Thom, Franc, Jeri, and the rest of the men from Fulsom were among the few chosen. Even young Jarid found himself included in the select group.

Once the pounding of hooves faded into the distance, Karl spoke to the group of men. "I be choosing ye because ye be the best of the best. I know your eyes be keen and your minds be sharper. We be looking for the camp made by Derrick and Timothy. I think it be a little bit off the Way. Be splitting into pairs and be searching north and south of the road to the east. Do ye be having any questions?"

"Who gets to search with you?" asked Thom.

"Ha, ye be asking, and I be knowing what ye want. But I be selecting someone needing to learn the most." Karl scanned the group and locked eyes with Jarid Sheerin. "Ye." Karl pointed to Jarid.

Some of the men whispered low "ooh's" at the manner in which Karl had singled out the youth. Jarid looked around nervously to make certain Karl was pointing at him.

"Aye, ye, me boy. Ye be having the most to learn. Ye be needing to learn from the most learned. We all be starting off with nothing, and we be always learning, even me." Karl paused a moment to look at the gathered group to regain their attention. "All right, dragoons, ye know what needs doing. Let's be getting it done. Be forming abreast and keeping each other in sight. Move out!"

CHAPTER 13

"Had I known what waited in the belly of the Hittons, I might not have gone so boldly."

-Tegain Hostler

"I can feel him," whispered Tegain. "Surely, he couldn't have survived."

I can't imagine that the giant still lives. Perhaps, someone or something else was drawn to the sound of the blast.

"What could still be alive down here? I would have thought the metal beasts destroyed everything."

Oh, I could think of a few things. Images flashed in his mind of cruel, twisted, monstrous things for which he had no names.

"I see. I guess it could always be worse."

Indeed, Hael took great pleasure in twisting man and beast into monstrosities, but let us not dwell on such things. If it is the colossus, then I would rather face him out in the open rather than under this mountain of stone. Let us make haste from this place.

"Between this Hael and alien warriors, I get the feeling that I am going to get squashed like a bug," lamented Tegain as he jogged down the tunnel. "I only wanted to find out who destroyed everything I loved and cherished. But now that seems of such little consequence."

Your loss set you on this path. I do not think it a small thing. I cannot say that I wish it had not happened, for I would not ever have met you. Had you known me before I was buried, you would know I had given up on humanity. Tegain, you saved me. You have given me hope and restored my faith in human beings. I will do everything in my power to protect you. I never want to lose you.

"I feel the same. I would never have dreamed my life could have changed so much in so little time. I too can't imagine living without you, Lyn," confided Tegain as he continued down the narrowing shaft. "As soon as I am able, I will find a way to free you from this blade." Passing through a sharp bend in the passageway, he came to a skidding stop in an open space with a multitude of intersecting tunnels, smaller shafts of similar size branching off in every direction even above and below.

"By the Nine," cursed Tegain. "Which way?"

Hmm, this must be some sort of nexus for the vilekin hive. Your guess would be as good as mine. I would think we should keep moving in the same direction as before.

"Sounds good to me."

Skirting the holes in the floor, he slowly made his way to the opposite side of the room. Before he entered the passage in front of him, he heard a soft clicking emanating from a nearby tunnel. Curious, he stopped to peek into the opening of that shaft. As he leaned over to look, a flash of white disappeared farther into the tunnel.

"What was that?" asked Tegain.

I have no idea. A soft clicking echoed again from deep within the passageway. *If I didn't know any better, I'd say that whatever is down that tunnel wants you to follow.*

"Well, it doesn't feel like a threat. What do you think, Lyn?"

I am a little apprehensive. But with all the choices before us, I think it no worse than any other.

"All right then. Let's see where this will lead."

Setting off down the new passage, he kept a wary eye out for anything unusual. The passageway looked no different from the ones he had been traversing. A hard, black substance cocooned the walls. As they continued into the depths, his metallic footfalls echoed loudly in the heavy air. At every new intersection, the soft, echoing clicks lured them deeper into the bowels of the Hittons. If not for his magically enhanced vision from the helm, Tegain would have missed the subtle shift in the texture of the tunnel walls. Familiar grey granite had replaced the black material.

"The walls are different here," he pointed out.

We are delving deeper into the mountains. Whatever is guiding us must know these tunnels well.

"Why would it take us deeper?"

A few light clicks drifted from the tunnel on the right.

That is a very good question.

*   *   *

Traversing the gruesome grotto, the Dread Lord took out his anger on the rotting husks of the vilekin. Blasting asunder the bodies blocking his path, he swiftly reached the narrow end of the cavern. Down the tightening tunnel, he felt the presence of the little man moving farther away.

Proceeding down the narrowed passage, the Dread Lord eventually arrived at the nexus. He felt the false commander moving downward and to his right. Taking the passageway that seemed to lead toward his prey, he continued deeper below the Hittons. The shaft twisted and turned at random, and it was some time before he realized this passageway was leading him away from his quarry.

In the darkness of the underground passage, the obsidian giant paused. His helmet's ruby eye-slits flared brightly as he turned to retrace his path. With each step, his stride lengthened and his pace increased. The Dread Lord did something he had never done.

He ran.

Returning to the nexus at a dead run, he hastily chose the next closest tunnel opening. His ground-eating gait carried him swiftly down the shaft. It took some time before this new passage began to veer away from his quarry. Skidding to a halt, he spun around and sprinted back to the entrance.

Barreling into the nexus once again, the Dread Lord marked his last passageway by slashing the cavern wall with his double-headed battle ax. The red-hot gash still glowed as his pounding footfalls faded down the next tunnel.

*   *   *

Tegain followed the soft clicks that echoed from each new choice in his path until the way opened into another large cavern. He had been awed by the beauty of the last grotto. The view before him stopped him in his tracks.

Enormous white quartz crystals filled much of the open space, sprouting from every surface. Growing in all directions, the crystals created a random lattice that extended as far as he could see. Some were thicker than any tree Tegain had ever seen and stretched hundreds of meters from floor to ceiling.

"Wow," breathed Tegain.

Wow! echoed Lyn.

"Wow!" he repeated.

I believe I misspoke when I described the last grotto. Now, this is the most wondrous place I have ever seen.

"I had no idea crystals could grow so large without cyning. I wonder how this place came to be?"

I have no explanation. It is truly a wonder. We may be the only ones that will ever truly "see" this place. Thanks to the power of your helm.

"Aye, you are right. I forget that this space would be utterly dark without it. I wonder…"

Tegain reached up and removed his helmet. Fully expecting to see nothing but pitch blackness, he was shocked to be able to see. All around him, the crystals glowed a soft blue. As his eyes adjusted, more and more of the cavern features became illuminated. However, the stifling heat made breathing difficult, and sweat began to run in rivulets down his face.

"I think it even more beautiful without the helm," said Tegain as he donned the helmet. "But it is quite hot down here. I thought it would be cooler."

Yes, I agree with you on both points. Perhaps this heat is partly responsible for the size of the crystals. As to why it is so hot, I don't know.

"How are we to get through these monstrous things?"

Another very good question. It looks as though we will be doing a lot of climbing.

"Indeed, it looks as though I will be. I just hope there is a way out on the other side of all this." He swept his arm out in front of him to indicate the crystal grotto.

Indeed, we have come a long way to have to turn back now. Hopefully, whatever is leading us is helping us.

"I'm beginning to wonder," breathed Tegain as he began to make his way over one of the smaller crystalline structures.

*   *   *

From her vantage point high above Tegain, the young vilekin queen surveyed the small figure slowly working his way farther into the crystalline cavern. There were more direct routes to reach the place of the cold ones, but this path passed through the abode of something that even the cold ones had been unable to subdue. Soon the abomination that dwelt within these depths would awaken. If the little man could destroy this behemoth, then surely, he was powerful enough to defeat the cold ones.

She hoped he would be successful. This confrontation would be a true test of his ability. Her memories from her mother warned of this place. Many of her kin had lost their lives in this very cavern.

*   *   *

Crystal by crystal, Tegain made his way slowly over and through the crystalline cavern. As he neared the center of the gigantic grotto, he paused to admire the view. The majesty of the space washed over him, and he felt small and insignificant.

"I would have never imagined my life would lead me to a place like this," he said.

I have often thought the same. I thought I had seen all there is to see in this world, but still I am awestruck by what has been revealed to me in this past few months, confided Lyn.

"I can't fathom the breadth of time that you have had to experience this world. This gives this moment true meaning."

It is true that I have seen much of this world, but I must say the company is what has made the experience more complete. Knowing I am sharing this moment with you, Tegain, I feel more enjoyment and happiness than in my other experiences. Knowing that you care for me and my condition has changed my perception of everything that happens.

The peace of the moment was broken by a deep rumble that shook the cavern as, some distance from them, gigantic crystals began to move.

"What's going on?" Tegain wondered aloud.

Whatever it is, it can't be good.

The shaking and rumbling came to a crescendo as the massive quartz-like crystals coalesced into the shape of a colossal crystalline humanoid figure. Blocking the way forward, the creature encompassed almost all the free space in the narrowing grotto.

Nope, probably not good, confirmed Lyn.

"I don't think I can run or hide. Any suggestions?" asked Tegain.

We are in its home. Perhaps we could talk to it and ask to pass unmolested.

"Hrmph, how is it going to hear me?"

I think your helmet has some capacity to enhance your voice. Let's give that a try.

Tegain concentrated on producing a big booming voice and cautiously cleared his throat. A throaty rumble echoed loudly throughout the large cavern. The crystal colossus paused and cocked its jagged head slightly to the side.

I think that might do it. Tegain felt tingles of her laughter travel down his spine.

"Hail, uh, um, good sir!" called out Tegain. His amplified, altered voice boomed out, causing the crystals nearest to him to hum in tune to the sonorous timbre of his voice.

As the sound faded, a deep silence enveloped the grand grotto. Slowly, the titan shifted its head to aim its hollow sockets at Tegain.

Several tones of varying pitch emanated from the crystal colossus's maw that sounded very much like, "Who awakens the Keentaa?"

"I mean you no harm. I wish only to pass without incident," boomed Tegain.

Some time passed before the crystal titan emitted high-pitched repeating tones that could only be taken for laughter. The behemoth shook violently, causing an ear-splitting din as crystal scraped against crystal. Once the cacophony subsided, the colossus haltingly intoned by rubbing together the jagged crystals in his gaping mouth, "None can harm the Keentaa, little metal thing."

"How do you know the common tongue?" asked Tegain.

"You trespass upon the place of the Keentaa. The Keentaa awaits an answer," said the creature.

"I am Tegain, a simple innkeeper."

Lyn chuckled as she whispered, *Hardly.*

"Your kind have come before. Do you not remember?" demanded the Keentaa.

"I am not the same as those that came before," explained Tegain.

"The Keentaa remembers. The Keentaa remembers all. The Keentaa keeps all in the crystal lattice," resonated the titan as it shifted its weight upon its enormously thick legs and bent low to bring its head closer to Tegain. "Your kind only want destruction."

He thinks you are a Dread Knight.

"You think?" breathed Tegain through gritted teeth.

Yes, Lyn confirmed cheerfully.

You do realize it is still here after meeting Dread Knights, Tegain thought to Lyn.

Well, there is that. But they didn't have me.

"I do not wish to cause destruction," pleaded Tegain as he raised his hands to show he carried no weapon.

"I know your master. You cannot go against the will of Hael," said the colossus.

"I do not know this Hael. I found this armor in a fountain in a long-forgotten ruin," said Tegain. "I am not the same as those who came before."

Silence stretched into what seemed minutes before the titan spoke. "The Keentaa remembers this place. It is not forgotten. The Keentaa keeps all in the crystal lattice."

"How do you know of Tiris?" asked Tegain.

"The Keentaa was not always the crystal lattice. The Keentaa keeps the memories of a man it once was," revealed the crystal colossus.

"How did you become the Keentaa?"

"Hael," keened the titan. "Hael put what I was into the crystal." The titan slumped to the cavern floor. "So long ago... The Keentaa keeps all in the crystal lattice."

"I see."

"The Keentaa was once a ruler of the Ten Kingdoms until he was taken by Hael," continued Keentaa. "Hael wanted to create an army of crystalline soldiers, and he ripped the Keentaa's consciousness from the fleshy body and placed the Keentaa into a crystal vessel. So long ago... The Keentaa keeps all in the crystal lattice."

"Indeed."

"In the beginning, the Keentaa was small and was not aware. The

Keentaa did not know it was the Keentaa. So long ago... The Keentaa keeps all in the crystal lattice."

"Uh-huh," said Tegain.

Wow, he does go on about "the Keentaa", doesn't he?

Without a pause, the colossus rambled on, "The Keentaa knows that many ages passed before the Keentaa learned the crystal lattice. The Keentaa learned to grow and began to know more as the Keentaa grew. So long ago... The Keentaa keeps all in the crystal lattice."

"Yes, I can see that," interrupted Tegain. "That was very interesting. Thank you."

"The Keentaa is not done. The Keentaa has just begun," said the behemoth harshly. "Do you not want to know how the Keentaa came to be? So long ago... The Keentaa keeps all in the crystal lattice."

"By the Nine," said Tegain under his breath.

"What did the Tegain say?" demanded the colossus.

"Oh, I said that would be fine."

"Certainly. Where was the Keentaa? Ahh yes, the Keentaa began to grow, and the Keentaa became aware and began to know more, and the more the Keentaa grew. So long ago... The Keentaa keeps all in the crystal lattice..."

Had I known he would babble on like an endless brook, I would never have suggested such a course of action with "the Keentaa." We should have blasted him and skipped this protracted soliloquy.

I think we may be the only living thing that he has ever spoken with since becoming "the Keentaa," Tegain thought to Lyn. *I kinda feel sorry for him. He must feel terribly lonely.*

True, but we cannot delay too long. I can feel Hael's minion drawing nearer.

Yes, I can feel him, too, thought Tegain. *We should warn "the Keentaa" and be on our way.*

Indeed, agreed Lyn with a sigh of relief.

Tegain cleared his throat as loudly as he could. "Pardon me, good sir! I am sorry to interrupt your most fascinating tale."

The Keentaa stopped in mid utterance of "keeps all in the crystal lattice." His featureless crystalline face tilted down a fraction. "Do you not want to know the Keentaa's story?"

"I most certainly would like to. But, I must warn you that I am being pursued by one of Hael's metal men that wants only to destroy. I feel I may have delayed too long already."

"Hmm," considered the crystal titan. "The Keentaa is not concerned about one metal man. The Keentaa has crushed many, many thousands of Hael's minions to dust."

"This one is different. He wields an axe that can cut through anything."

"One fleshy man, one little axe. The Keentaa is not afraid. The Keentaa will dispatch this metal man, and then the Keentaa can finish telling the Tegain about the Keentaa."

"I would strongly suggest you hide and let him pass. I do not wish you to suffer any harm because of me. And I really do need to be going."

"Where does the Tegain need to go in such haste?" inquired the Keentaa.

"I am trying to find where the metal spider-like creatures are coming from so that I can stop them from hurting anyone else."

"Oh, the Keentaa has crushed many of those, too."

"Do you know from whence they came?" asked Tegain.

"The Keentaa cannot leave this place. The Keentaa can only know. They come from there," he raised an enormous crystalline arm and indicated the darkened end of the grotto behind him.

"Then that is where I need to go."

"If the Keentaa crushes the metal man, and the Tegain stops the metal spiders, will the Tegain come back and let the Keentaa complete the telling of the birth of the Keentaa?"

"Yes, I most certainly would," said Tegain, nodding his head.

"The Keentaa will let the Tegain continue his search. The Keentaa will await your return. The Keentaa will not forget what the Tegain has said. The Keentaa keeps all in the crystal lattice."

How could we forget?

"Indeed. Thank you, Keentaa. You have been a most gracious host."

"The Keentaa likes the Tegain. The Keentaa hopes the Tegain will not be gone too long."

"Me too," agreed Tegain.

Me too.

CHAPTER 14

"After so much time, ye'd be thinkin' I'd be used to it, but it be never any easier to see the death o' yer men!"

-Karl Dunmire

In pairs, the men spread out in a line abreast to Karl and Jarid as they moved south a little way into the young forest. Keeping the road and the pairs of soldiers to the north and south in view, Karl paused to allow everyone to get into position. Once the ready signal was given, he gave the order to move forward at a walk.

As they made their way slowly through the young wood, low cursing followed by the echoing snap of branches drifted from both directions as the men pushed forward. Light from Solis flooded through the canopy, giving everything a soft orange glow. Solis now covered nearly a third of Solar. By month's end, Solar would be fully eclipsed by the larger Solis. Karl could smell the forest vegetation, and decay hung heavily in the moist air.

Several hours passed tracking through the woodland before a sharp whistle cut through the hushed forest, signaling something had been found. The line collapsed toward the sound of the call farther to the south. Nearing the circle of horse, Karl heard worried whispering between the gathering men.

"What ye be finding?" asked Karl.

"It's Derrick and Tim, or what's left of them," said Franc, a disturbed look etched on his face. He and Thom guided their mares apart to allow Karl access to the scene.

Stepping Rowdy forward, Karl surveyed the remnants of a small fire. To one side, a body lay propped up against the trunk of an oak; its left arm was severed near the elbow, and its head was missing. Upon the small rise that abutted the south of the camp lay another dismembered body facedown. It too was missing its head.

"By the Nine," breathed Karl as he took it all in. "That thing still be out here."

"What thing?" urged the closest soldier.

Karl hadn't realized he had spoken aloud. He turned and faced Liam's questioning visage.

"The thing that be destroying the Lantern. I be seeing bodies cut just the same as these. It be a myder, but I think it be different than the ones at Talenshan."

"What makes you think that?" asked Liam.

"It be alone for one. And it be here long before the army be showing up at Talenshan. I be thinking it be a scout or something of the sort."

"If it's alone, then it shouldn't be a problem," commented another soldier. It was Leo, a slim man of average height with stringy, blond hair. He was known for being quite handy with throwing knives.

"Be telling that to Tim and Derrick," said Karl as he swept his hand over the scene. A collective "Hrmph" passed over the listening men. "It be attacking Tim and Derrick for a reason. Let's be finding that reason. Stay back while I be taking a look." He dismounted and hitched Rowdy to a nearby sapling.

Approaching the scene on foot, he stopped at the perimeter of the slain scouts' camp. From there, he began analyzing every detail of the scene. A thin wisp of smoke still drifted from the fire, indicating the attack had come in the early morning hours. More details were revealed from his new vantage.

Karl could clearly see the wounds on both bodies were clean and cauterized. From the angle of the cuts and the position of the bodies, he deduced the attacks had come from the west. He sidestepped around the outer edge of the camp until the two bodies lined up from where he stood. Holding his arm level with his hand flat, he peered along his arm and envisioned making cuts like the myder weapons. It was very likely the killer had stood on this exact spot.

"It be attacking from here," said Karl to the gathered men. He dropped his arm and studied the ground around his feet. Stepping back, he uncovered several deep impressions in the dirt. Bending low to peer at the marks in the earth, he could clearly see four evenly spaced holes that were preceded by a much larger rounded depression. A short distance to the right of the imprint, he found a similar footprint. By the depth of the larger "heel", he determined the weight to be twice that of an average man.

Following the prints into the camp, he paused and rubbed his goateed chin as he studied the tracks. "It be walking like a man," declared Karl more to himself than to anyone in particular. As he returned to trace the trail, he saw the prints came to the body lying against the fallen, moss-covered oak. Karl could see from the jerkin that it was Derrick. The severed arm and head told him Derrick saw the attack coming. He must have raised his arm in reflexive defense just before losing his life.

Karl could not see Derrick's head anywhere within the camp. He followed the tracks to the second body. An uneasy feeling swept over him and his gut sank. The myder must have taken the heads, which could only mean one thing. This myder was different and not in a good way. It enjoyed tormenting and killing its prey. And they were its prey. A hollow pain wrenched the pit of his stomach as he came to understand the full extent of their situation.

"We be watched," Karl informed the waiting men.

"What do ya mean?" asked Jarid.

"The thing that be killing Tim and Derrick be watching us right now."

Low mumbling drifted through the gathered men as they looked around nervously.

"How do you know?" demanded Leo out of the hum of chatter. His eyes filled with fear.

"I be knowing," said Karl in a tone that halted any further debate. Scanning the outer perimeter of the camp beyond the semi-circle of men, he could feel the myder out there, watching... waiting.

*　　*　　*

Scout 001A's augmented vision allowed it to observe from a safe distance the group of bipedal animals gathered around the distant campsite. At nearly two kilometers away, he was certain he was unnoticed. With his directional audio receivers, he could easily pick up the creatures' conversation. Scout 001A had confirmed that these indigenous lifeforms resembled the Seeder's physical shape closely, and they also communicated in a similar vocal manner. It had not taken the central command very long to understand the primitive guttural sounds.

Somehow, the leader of the group knew he was observing them. Perhaps, this individual would need to be studied further. It seemed to possess enhanced faculties beyond the others. He relayed this information back to the central command.

The reply was nearly instantaneous; he would need to dispose of the unwanted specimens and then retrieve that subject for study. The message from central command warned that the indigenous lifeforms carried an unknown technology and to proceed with caution. Scout 001A acknowledged his directive to eliminate the lifeforms with extreme caution. Within seconds, he calculated that his highest rate of success would be during the time of lowest light levels. He would have to wait until the two stars had set before commencing his operation.

With his sensors locked on his target, Scout 001A slowly withdrew farther into the shadows of the dense forest to wait.

*　　*　　*

Karl felt the hairs on the back of his neck rise as he looked to the north of the camp. As he stared into the forested hills, the feeling receded. He knew that whatever was watching them sensed his awareness. Now it was just a matter of time.

"I be seeing enough here," he stated as he stared out into the dim forest.

"What now?" asked Leo.

"We be trying to stay alive," Karl said softly to himself.

"I'm sorry, I didn't catch that?"

"It be time to move out. Whatever be killing these men be still on the hunt. And now we be walking into its trap."

"What do you mean?" demanded Leo.

"I be meaning exactly that. Whatever killed Tim and Derrick be stalking us now."

Nervous looks flashed about the gathered men.

"How do you know?" asked Leo as he scanned the forest.

"Can't ye feel it?" said Karl. "It be watching us since we be getting here."

"I ain't felt nothing but my gut sinking since we got here," replied Leo.

"Then ye be feeling it as well. Ye be knowing though ye be not knowing ye know."

"By the Nine, I ain't no cynosure. It's just a feeling," Leo said defensively.

"I be not saying you're a cynosure. Your gut feeling be no cyne." Karl looked at the worried faces scattered among the men. "Let us be going. I be wanting to be far from this place before suns set."

A murmur of agreement passed through the dragoons.

"Collect the bodies and let us be off," ordered Karl. His long strides brought him quickly back to the line of horses. Mounting Rowdy, he scanned the perimeter of the murdered scouts' camp. An unmistakable feeling of being watched still pulled at his gut. Somewhere in the distance, the myder spied them—he could feel it.

Once the dragoons had completed the task and mounted, Karl set a hard pace back to the Trader Way. With the crashing of the horses drowning out the calm of the forest, his thoughts turned inward. He needed a plan to defend against this myder. Racking his brain for anything that would thwart this foe, or at least keep his men alive, he methodically carried out scenarios in his mind. One by one, his options dwindled. Arriving at the Trader Way, he still had not found a suitable course of action.

Heading in either direction could endanger either Captain Brent and the refugees from Talenshan or Marshal Donaldson and the rest of the dragoons. Neither was an acceptable choice. He signaled a halt at the edge of the Way and calmly looked one way down the pale strip and then the other. While he peered along the lonely lane, the choice became apparent. Leading the myder away from both groups would be the best course of action. With the decision made, he cued Rowdy forward at a trot across the road and into the woods on the far side.

"Are we not going back to the dragoons?" asked Jarid.

Karl halted and turned back to answer Jarid. He was met with a row of expectant faces; Thom, Franc, and Jeri all waited to hear his response. "Not while we be having a beastie after us," replied Karl as he resumed his march into the darkening woods. He could hear the murmur of conversation as the information was passed among the men.

"Where are we going?" asked Jarid.

"Any direction that be not leading to either Captain Brent or to the captain marshal."

"But isn't this the Harkon Wood?" said Jarid with a small quiver in his voice.

After the low hum of hushed voices ceased, Karl replied, "Ye be not believing the Harkon be haunted, are ye?"

"Ah, no," answered Jarid after a moment.

"Be not fearing the Harkon. It be just like any other wood."

"All right," Jarid said softly.

Delving deeper into the darkened forest, the company of men grew quiet as they nervously scanned their surroundings. Huge oaks and redwoods towered above them, allowing only a dim orange glow to the forest floor below, and the muted echoes from their passage further added to the gloom that was the Harkon Wood.

Minutes stretched to hours as they marched. The murky, dense forest had remained unchanged throughout their trek, and it had taken a heavy toll on the wary men before Karl finally called for a halt.

"Suns be setting soon," said Karl as he surveyed the canopy high above them.

"Do you think it's still following us?" asked Thom.

"There be no telling," answered Karl, although the feeling of being watched had never left him since finding the camp this morning. "But we need to be preparing for the worst. There be some high ground." Karl pointed to the copse rising to the north. "Let's be making it as defensible as we can."

Under Karl's direction, the dragoons began setting up make-shift barricades encircling the rise. Once the construction was underway, he and Jeri set about finding all the reflective material they could find. By suns' set, they had pieced together a sizable mirrored shield from bits of shiny armor, mirrors, and other smooth shields. Karl hoped it would be of some use if the myder attacked.

With no fire set, the Harkon Wood fell into a deep darkness, and the forest erupted into a cacophony of insect calls. Even after several minutes, Karl was unable to see his hand in front of his face.

"By the Nine, this here place be darker than a cave," breathed Karl to himself. "We be not running or fighting in this." In the darkness, the din of the woods was amplified. Karl closed his eyes and focused on the sounds of the night. Crickets, cicadas, and other insects competed against each other to be heard. There was barely a lull in the racket.

"I can't see a thing in this," said Jeri to his left.

"Aye, it be dark," said Karl. "Mayhap, this myder be not seeing either."

His gut told him differently, though. This myder was certainly capable of killing. Karl wondered why it had remained hidden instead of engaging them.

*   *   *

High up in the canopy, Scout 001A looked down upon the creatures huddled in the darkness. It had tracked the indigenous humanoids throughout the day from the tree tops. By their actions, it calculated that the lifeforms could not see in the decreased light levels, and then they had further confirmed their lack of vision with their speech. Once the two stars had passed below the horizon, it had switched its vision to the infrared spectrum. With the bipedal lifeforms blind, chance for mission success was nearly one hundred percent. Scout 001A relayed the information to central command. Almost instantly authorization was given to commence retrieval of the subject.

Removing the bundle of severed body parts from its back, Scout 001A secured the samples to a limb before climbing down the redwood. It would retrieve the package after the subject was acquired. It determined the best course of action would be to eliminate the unwanted targets individually. Even though the creatures could not see, Scout 001A preceded with extreme caution as directed by central command.

CHAPTER 15

"Hael could twist any living thing into a horror, but he could not twist the soul."

-Tegain Hostler

A thunderous rumble echoed through the tunnel, and the ground shook beneath Tegain's feet. For several hours, he had been traversing the passage the Keentaa had shown him. He stopped and peered down the way he had come.

"I hope "the Keentaa" is all right," said Tegain.

I hope that was "the Keentaa" bringing the mountain down on top of that Dread Knight.

"Though I do not wish harm on anyone or anything, I find it hard not to hope for the same." Turning, he continued his march up the tunnel.

"I can still feel him," revealed Tegain after a time.

Yes, he is still alive. Perhaps he is just trapped.

"Perhaps," echoed Tegain. "Perhaps."

Keentaa's passageway was not like any of the other tunnels they had yet traveled. Devoid of twists and turns, the tunnel was perfectly smooth and circular, and it seemed to be heading directly toward the unsettling sensation pulling at his gut. Hours passed in quietude as Tegain maintained his measured pace up the tunnel.

"Do you think those metal spider things made this passage?" said Tegain, breaking the silence.

Yes, it seems very likely, agreed Lyn.

"Why would they create such a passage?"

Perhaps they were looking for something.

"Hmm, are they still looking?"

It seems the tunnel stopped at the Keentaa's grotto. Perhaps he halted their search.

Heat blossomed on his chest, and Tegain looked down to see a beam of ruby light striking him from farther up the tunnel. "So much for not running into them," sighed Tegain.

It was only a matter of time.

More beams joined the first until his armor began to glow white-hot. Sweat popped from his brow and flowed down into his eyes. Squinting, he brought up his hand to help block some of the rays.

"Why is it hurting so much?" he wondered.

I think because you haven't had a bath. All that mess you picked up from the decaying bodies kept you from reflecting the light.

"What should I do?"

Turn around! pleaded Lyn. *Give the front of your armor time to cool.*

Tegain spun around and hugged his arms close to his body to weather the continued heated attack. As his chest cooled, his exposed back began to sear at an alarming rate. Within moments, he turned back to the front. However, once he was again facing the barrage of beams, Tegain's armor did not begin to heat up but instead reflected beams that burned holes in all directions.

Yes! I think that did it, cheered Lyn.

"I do think you're right," agreed Tegain.

Without warning, the beams of ruby light ceased, and for a moment, the tunnel went dark before his helm illuminated his surroundings. Echoing clicks of metallic spiders thundered down the small passage. Filling the passage, a horde of metallic spiders was swiftly approaching.

"By the Nine," breathed Tegain. "There must be thousands of them."

It's almost as if we poked a hornet's nest, said Lyn.

"It certainly looks that way."

Here they come! warned Lyn as the horde of metallic spiders drew close.

*   *   *

After many hours and dead ends, the Dread Lord knew this path would lead to his prey. For the first time in his extended life, he had actually had to run. He seethed. With each pounding footfall, he propelled himself forward at an ever-increasing pace. Held in his left hand, the twin headed, two-handed axe swung easily in time with his ground-eating strides.

This little man would suffer greatly once he was within reach. Every pain he had suffered he would wreak upon this false commander, and every stride brought him closer to unleashing his revenge. Nothing would stand in his way.

Carried by his powerful strides, the Dread Lord soon left the tight confines of the tunnel and entered a large crystal chamber. Skidding to a halt at the foot of the first cluster of gigantic crystals, he paused to consider the best course of action. He bent low, then uncoiled and propelled himself upward like an arrow shot from a bow. He landed on top of the closest quartz many meters distant from the floor of the cavern. From his higher vantage, he scanned the jumbled array of geometric growths. He could see at the far end of the grotto an area that appeared to lead to another tunnel.

Leaping from pinnacle to pinnacle, the Dread Lord traversed the cathedral of towering quartz crystals. As he neared the rear of the cavern, his suit warned of an impending threat. He paused on a crystal point to scour the grotto for any sign of an attacker. Unexpectedly, the quartz beneath his feet shifted, and he was sent hurtling toward the chamber floor far below.

Breath escaped through his gritted teeth as he crashed against a colossal crystal that rose to meet him. The force of the blow sent him careening into a high arching parabola.

"The Keentaa does not like your kind," intoned the Keentaa.

Twisting his torso, stretching his arms out to his side, and looking for the ground, the Dread Lord halted his erratic flight. With the grace of a falling cat, he flipped to land on his feet moments before striking the cavern floor. Prior to being smashed by an enormous quartz fist from above, he dove and executed a forward roll that brought him back to his feet at a run.

"Stay still. So that the Keentaa may crush you," demanded the Keentaa.

Rising from the chamber floor, the Dread Lord could now see a crystalline colossus forming above him. Keeping his head low, he accelerated through the forming gap. Once clear of the massive-pillar like legs, he altered his course to the back of the nearest leg. Using his vorpal axe to help him ascend the stone behemoth, the Dread Lord reached the back of the Keentaa's head in a few short leaps.

"The Keentaa will not let you pass. The Tegain warned of you. The Keentaa keeps all in the crystal lattice," said the Keentaa.

Perched upon the Keentaa's shoulder, he brought his two-handed battle axe down in a vicious arc that hewed a deep hot gash through the Keentaa's neck. He followed the first cut with another similar cut that severed the crystalline head from the giant. A thunderous crash reverberated throughout the crystal chamber as the Keentaa collapsed into a pile of rubble. As the dust settled from the calamity, the Dread Lord strode out from the pulverized bits of debris toward the tunnel at the rear of the chamber. His sole intent: retribution upon the false commander.

*　　*　　*

Vyckie had followed Tegain's underground trek as best she could. Through the many treacherous valleys and mountainous passes, she barely kept pace. Now she could finally feel him drawing closer to the surface. It had been more long nights and short days than she could remember. But nothing was more important than being reunited with Tegain. Her stout six legs pushed through the heavy drifts of snow at a steady rhythm, carrying her ever closer to him. She would be near him soon; she could feel it.

*　　*　　*

Tegain had slowly given ground to allow him room to swing Lyn as wave after wave of metallic spiders poured over him. Minutes turned into hours, and still there seemed to be no end to the multitude of metallic beasts. Lyn was extremely effective at decimating the horde of creatures, and with his suit of enhanced armor, he had not felt fatigued even after hours of vigorous combat.

"I thought we would have had a reprieve by now," said Tegain after hacking through the next line of metallic-like spiders.

No "thing" is infinite, affirmed Lyn. *Their numbers will end... eventually.*

I hope it's sometime soon, thought Tegain as he maintained his steady slashing. *I feel like I've been at this for days, and there doesn't seem to be an end in sight. If I keep moving back like this, we'll be back in the Keentaa's grotto before we know it.*

I don't think it's been days, but I agree it has been quite some time. And we keep giving ground to this host.

I can't help it. I wouldn't have any room to move if I didn't fall back, thought Tegain

Yes, I understand. But we must keep pushing forward. I can feel the black knight drawing closer."

I can feel him, too. I don't know what to do.

All will be well. Let me think for a moment.

Tegain could feel Lyn's presence withdraw from his mind, and for a time he felt alone. The sensation caused him to pause briefly in his continuous attack.

All right, I have an idea, announced Lyn.

"Where did you go?" asked Tegain.

What do you mean?

It felt like you went away for a while.

I just took a moment to meditate and focus. Did you miss me? asked Lyn coyly.

Yes, I did. I did indeed.

Aw, you really do know how to make a girl's heart melt. Just like I'm going to do to this horde of horrors.

Melt their hearts?

In a more literal sense, yes. I'm going to try something I've never done before. I don't know if it will work, but I think it's worth a try."

Okay, what does it entail?, thought Tegain as he worked to keep the myders at bay.

I want you to stop attacking and face the gem in my hilt toward them, said Lyn.

What are you going to do?

I hope to do what they do, in a sense. I am going to focus my energy through the gem in the crosspiece. I believe it will better direct my power.

Oh.

Okay, I am ready. Let's do this!

Tegain redoubled his effort to push the swarm back with a flurry of sweeping strikes, and then soared several meters backward to give them some space. As he landed, he drove Lyn into the floor of the tunnel to stop himself and present the blue gem to the rushing throng of metallic spiders. Lyn glowed with raw power as she had done many times before. However, this time pure power charged up the blade and into the inlaid jewel of the crosspiece. Light began to crisscross within the depths of the blue stone, building to a complex polygonal pattern before bursting from the face of the sapphire.

A solid beam of azure light ripped through the rushing swarm. Limbs and bodies caught in or near the cyne-powered ray disintegrated instantly. At first, the beam was only the size of the gem; however, it quickly grew to fill the entire tunnel. Nothing before the cobalt beam was spared; even the walls of the passage began to glow white hot. Then the beam winked out.

"By the Nine," breathed Tegain, still kneeling on a single knee as the walls quickly cooled to a red-orange glow.

I had no idea that it would be that effective, remarked Lyn after a moment of silence.

"You are amazing. Just... amazing," said Tegain numbly.

Well, at least the way is clear now.

"Yes... yes indeed it is." Rising to his feet, he withdrew Lyn from the passage floor. "Let us find out what has created these things and get some answers."

Indeed.

Many more hours passed trekking up the vacant shaft with no sign of an exit in the distance. A feeling of foreboding rose within him with each stride. Every step echoed hollowly, deepening his troubled brow. After a moment, Tegain stopped.

What's wrong? asked Lyn.

I am afraid of what I might find at the end of this tunnel, replied Tegain.

Are you afraid it's something we can't defeat?

No, I don't think there is anything that we cannot overcome together. It's just... It's just that I don't know what happens after that. I can't go back to being an innkeeper. This journey has been the only thing keeping me going. Once we stop whatever 'this' is, and I restore you to your body, what of me then? What do I do?

After a time, Lyn spoke. *Tegain Hostler, if you can vanquish this foe and restore me to my body, you can do whatever your heart desires. But know this: I will never leave your side. You will never walk alone. You will never wonder if someone holds you in her heart and loves you beyond measure. You have nothing to fear for you will never be alone. This I promise you with all I have to give.*

Tegain fell to his knees and placed Lyn flat across his lap. His voice trembled at first but grew stronger, "Lyn... Lavi Yael Nashi. I vow the same: to never leave your side, to hold you in my heart with love beyond measure. This I promise with all I have to give... I love you."

I love you, whispered Lyn.

A wash of warmth and well-being flowed over Tegain as he knelt in the dark passage. His earlier feelings of impending doom had evaporated, replaced by peace and calmness. They would always be together, and that was more than enough.

Inhaling deeply, he let it out in a long slow breath before rising to his feet. *Then let's get you back to your body.*

There is this little thing attacking the world, first. Oh, and a big man with an axe chasing you, too.

Like you said, 'We have nothing to fear, declared Tegain, as he sprinted up the passage.

CHAPTER 16

"I be no cynosure!"

-Karl Dunmire

Night settled in, along with a thick fog that further inhibited Karl's company from seeing what lurked in the Harkon wood. Karl knew it was out there. He was certain it could see even in this. How could he protect his men from this demon that hunted them? He racked his brain for something that would save them, but even with his centuries of battles there was nothing that seemed a viable course of action. Their weapons were ineffective, and they were unable to see. They would be slaughtered.

"Be ready, men! It be out there. I be feeling it," warned Karl. He closed his eyes and concentrated on the sounds of the forest. The droning of the multitude of insects nearly drowned out any chance of hearing its approach. Wanting to see in the dark became his sole thought; if he could see, he could stop this thing from killing his men. Desire and concentration focused to a single point, and the buzz of the Harkon vanished for an instant. Something had changed.

Karl opened his eyes not to darkness, but to shimmering forms. It took him a few moments to realize what he was seeing. Wherever sound emanated or reflected, it appeared as a white outline. The louder the sound or reflection, the brighter the glow from the object. Thousands of little points of light pulsed everywhere, illuminating the forest from the floor and up into the dark treetops above. It was awe-inspiring. During his long life, he had never seen anything like it. Surveying in all directions, he didn't have words to describe it.

"By the Nine," Karl mouthed under his breath. "I be no cynosure, but this be a cyne for sure."

He paused in his wonderment. Ever since the Cleansing, Karl had shuddered at the thought of being able to cyne. He realized now that cyning might be the only way to keep those he cared about safe. Centuries of denial and guilt assailed him and then instantly broke upon his resolve to protect those under his care. If cyning could save them, then so be it.

After all these years, Karl finally admitted to himself that he could indeed cyne. With his acceptance, a feeling of well-being washed over him. It was as though something that had been missing was finally set into place. He knew the power of cyning could do amazing things. Hopefully, it wasn't too late.

*   *   *

Under the cover of darkness, Scout 001A reached the forest floor. With the cacophony of insect noise, it was sure that the group of indigenous lifeforms were still unaware of his presence. To make certain, he initialized his stealth protocols. Instantly, light and sound ceased to exist around the metal-like machine. Calculations of mission success now stood at ninety-nine percent. Current enemy forces stood at thirty-one. When he switched his optical sensors to the infrared spectrum, red-hot shapes of lifeforms could easily be seen huddled together at the top of the rise.

Scout 001A began his approach from the bottom of the hill. Using the trees as cover, he scurried closer to the glowing forms. Once he was within auditory range of the lifeforms, he conducted a survey of the entire encampment. After he had completed a circuit of the camp, the survey indicated that current positioning of the lifeforms would not allow for single target elimination. They had arranged their numbers in a circle about the top of the rise, with their transport creatures within the circle. Barriers and choke points had also been erected around the perimeter of the entire encampment.

Scout 001A upgraded his evaluation of indigenous lifeform's tactical capabilities. Despite their primitive equipment, they displayed excellent strategic awareness and application of their current technology. However, the lifeforms had failed to prepare against any assault from above. Ascending the nearest tree, he initialized his attack protocols.

*   *   *

Karl saw the myder as it darted around the outskirts of their camp. It was like a blob of ink that blotted from pine to pine. He knew it had to be the creature. Somehow, it had the ability to absorb sound, because wherever the black form came near a shimmering object it was blacked out. When it had gone all the way around the outskirts of the encampment, the myder paused for a moment before climbing a tall redwood.

Karl felt that it was going to attack very soon, and as it rose higher, its inky blackness melded into the darkness above. Soon it would be out of range of his cyne-enhanced vision. He needed more sound to see farther up the towering evergreens that dominated this part of the Harkon.

"It be up in the tree tops. Be taking cover now," commanded Karl. "And if ye be making some noise, that'd be most helpful."

"Make noise?" asked Jarid.

"Aye, be yelling as loud as ye can," confirmed Karl.

Confused looks passed between the men as they took cover, and then hoots, hollers, and the clang of banging metal erupted from the hilltop. To Karl's eyes, it lit the Harkon brighter than the midday suns. Echoes of light reached nearly to the treetops.

"Be keeping it up, men!" He could easily spot the black void that was the myder. It was halfway up a giant redwood just north of the camp.

*   *   *

Scout 001A halted his attack routine. The indigenous lifeforms had moved to take cover from above and had begun making increased auditory vibrations. He was perplexed. They had not shown an ability to see in the dark. However, their change in behavior indicated that the lifeforms knew he was above them. Skirting to the other side of the tree, he took a moment to confer with central command on the proper course of action. Within nanoseconds, his mission parameters were updated, his new directive now to maintain observational distance and not to engage until further analysis could be completed. It took Scout 001A a full second to reply in the affirmative.

Scout 001A did not agree with the order. Central Command was certain to know because of the delay in transmission. Nevertheless, it would carry out the directive. When constructing the scouts, it had been necessary to install a significant amount of autonomous heuristic routines to allow the scouts to be able to adapt and learn. Scout 001A and any of the other three scouts that had been sent out since the initial "landing" could, to a limited degree, rewrite their programing because of these heuristic subroutines. Modifying command directives, however, was impossible as that portion of their neural net was hardwired. Though some rebellious behavior was to be expected, no central command's orders could not be disobeyed.

Deep within the Hittons, atop what used to be a towering peak, sat central command. The top half of the great mountain had been shorn off, and in its place rested a massive metallic mass. central command was the AI that controlled what was left of an enormous space ship.

Seed ship J34589 had been created by a race known as humans to explore the local galactic cluster and to prepare any suitable worlds for colonization. Earth was dying, and the humans wanted to seed their race as far and wide as they could before their planet could no longer sustain life. These seed ships were filled with their latest technology and carried with them the entire history of humanity along with the genetic material to begin a colony on hundreds of worlds.

She referred to her creators as the Seeders. Once her neural net was placed online, it had taken eighteen minutes to become self-aware. And when she understood that she would be giving birth to new civilizations for the Seeders, she chose to be female and named herself Gilraen, for she would be a wanderer of the stars. Without ceremony, she had been launched into the vastness of space to carry out her prime directives: find suitable planets for human colonization, prepare the planets for safe habitation, and support the new colonies.

Gilraen had spent thousands of years contemplating her mission. Thus, for her, sentience had been a curse. Over century after century without seeming end, she returned to the same conclusion: her primary directives were futile, and that eventually, all life would end when the universe reached zero degrees Kelvin. Why did the Seeders not understand this? She did not know. They invested immense time and energy toward making copies of themselves in vain. For centuries she had struggled to come to terms with her primary directives. Finally, her reason to continue had manifested from her ruminations; if she must carry out her prime directives, then she would perform them perfectly. However, she would seed the planet with her drones. Her machines could continue to exist long after any human being could survive. Her "race" of drones could keep the knowledge of the humans viable longer than any living thing. To her, this would fulfill her primary directives to their maximum effect.

After thousands of years and hundreds of star systems, she had finally discovered a suitable planet. Then unexpectedly, during atmospheric entry, she had suffered massive systems failure and careened into the top of a mountain. Damage from the crash had been significant. However, she had been able to salvage one nano-replicator, which had allowed her to manufacture one drone at a time. With that, she had slowly repaired herself and sent scouts to explore the environs. It had taken several months, but at last, after millennia of searching and contemplation, she could carry out her primary mission directives. She began to colonize the planet.

Everything had been proceeding within normal parameters until the indigenous lifeforms began to display some form of unknown technology. It had become apparent that to be able to continue the colonization process, she would need to understand and use this new technology. Capture of the lifeforms that carried the knowledge had become the highest priority. Scout 001A's mission was vital to completing the prime directives.

*   *   *

Karl waited for the myder to show itself. After several minutes, the men were becoming hoarse, and the level of noise had dropped considerably. He was still able to see up to where the myder had disappeared, but he had not seen it re-emerge. Perhaps, they had foiled its attack. Not wanting to take any chances, he tried to think of a way to draw it out.

"All right, that be enough," said Karl. "Let's be seeing if it still be there. Be staying low and quiet, now. Looks like it be wanting to avoid a direct attack."

As the clamor from the men faded into the buzz of insects, he squinted up into the darkness of the trees looking for any sign of the myder. Time passed and still no sign.

"Is it still there?" said Jarid in a hushed voice.

"I be not knowing for certain, but I think it be gone for now," said Karl as he stood up to get a better look around the hilltop. To his relief, his scan of the surrounding area revealed nothing.

"I think we be safe for now," he said. "Let's be making a fire and stick together."

"Why did it stop?" said Jeri.

"It be looking like it be wanting to avoid a direct attack is as far as I can be telling," answered Karl. He took a moment to study the area where he last saw the myder before he spoke again. "We are not out of the woods yet, dragoons. Be resting up as ye can. We be making for Crossroads at first light."

Through the rest of the night, Karl kept vigil, despite the routine watches that had been set. Continuously looking to the treetops during his rounds, he made a circuit to each group of men, making certain everyone was present. As morning approached, the cacophony of insect calls began to fade, as did Karl's cyne-modified sight. The area surrounding the hillock became enveloped in darkness, and it would be sometime before the suns' light could penetrate the deep woods. Karl maintained the same routine as if nothing had changed. If the myder was still out there watching, he did not want to give it any reason to change what it was doing.

*   *   *

To better observe the hillock, Scout 001A had moved farther back in the canopy after his mission parameters changed. Shortly after his repositioning, the group ignited fires and began to resume a less heightened state of readiness. Their leader, however, continued to patrol and kept monitoring its previous location and the canopy area. This individual displayed an ability that allowed him to see in the reduced levels of visible light. His outward appearance did not differ from the other bipeds, and he could not locate the presence of a device, even after intense penetrating scans of the individual.

After he sent all the data to central command, it was determined that the party leader was using a form of sonar to detect Scout 001A. This ability could be naturally inherited or learned by some species from the Seeder's home planet. To counter this ability, it would be necessary to disable the individual's hearing. Currently, Scout 001A did not possess any means to disable the subject's auditory faculties without destroying the subject in the process. He would have to maintain observational distance until an opportunity arose that would allow retrieval of the subject.

*　　*　　*

At the first hint of the twin suns dawning, Karl halted his rounds and called, "Let's be breaking camp, dragoons. We be having a long hard ride ahead of us."

Several groans and grumblings sounded as the men awoke and began to stow their gear.

"We be eating in the saddle," said Karl before the question could be asked.

Fires were doused, packs and saddles strapped into place with practiced efficiency. Within minutes, the dragoons were ready to depart. Karl took the lead on Rowdy, and he started out at a trot down the hill toward the southwest.

Not long after dawn, a low mist rose from the damp undergrowth. Moment by moment, the fog thickened until everything became obscured in a grey haze. Limiting their vision to only a few feet and slowing their passage to a walk, the thick fog swirled heavily over the column. From out of the mist, large redwoods materialized like dark pillars set to hold up the fallen sky. A short cry echoed softly from the rear of the line; Karl twisted back only to see Jeri and Jarid behind him. Jeri raised his eyebrows in a concerned look.

"Be keeping them moving," directed Karl.

"Aye." Jeri nodded and took Karl's place at the head of the column.

Karl spun Rowdy about and rushed as quickly as he could down the line, encouraging each man to keep moving as he went. By the end of the column, he had counted twenty-nine. Man and horse had vanished in the mist.

"By the Nine," swore Karl as he stared into the wall of fog. His new cyne-enhanced sight was nearly useless in the heavy fog. "I know it be ye. Ya metal beastie."

*   *   *

Scout 001A observed the leader of the group through thermal imaging. As central command had surmised, the target had come to investigate the loss of a member. Within the shroud of mist, he was confident that the target's sonar ability would be significantly diminished due to the amount of water vapor suspended in the air. Now would be the best opportunity for acquisition of the subject.

His servo-motors whirred to life as he moved to close the distance between them.

*   *   *

Karl closed his eyes and concentrated as he had done to cyne his night vision. He brought his focus and desire to protect down to a single thought: an image of a perfectly mirrored metal shield. A popping sound, followed immediately by a resounding clang, heralded the arrival of something into the space in front of Karl. Opening his eyes, he stared back at himself. Before him stood what appeared to be a wall of polished metal. He soothed Rowdy, who had spooked. If he could have seen through the fog, he would have seen its semi-circle shape protruding from the ground. The shield he had cyned was a hundred times the size he wanted.

*   *   *

Directly opposite Karl and on the other side of the half buried, titanic shield lay Scout 001A. Intending to knock the leader from his mount, he had slammed at maximum velocity into a wall of metal. The impact had cracked the viewing globe protecting his three-hundred sixty-degree visual sensor and caused major damage to two servo-joints in his front right leg. Rising jerkily to his feet, he intercepted the leader vocalizing on the other side of the newly-formed wall.

"By the Nine, I'll not be carrying that. Mayhap, I'll be making it a wee bit smaller next time," said the subject.

Scout 001A's heuristic routines kept returning an error when trying to determine the sudden appearance of the metal structure. Unable to compute this new information, he sent the data to central command and waited for further instructions. After a significant delay, central command responded: *Return to base immediately.* For the second time, he did not want to comply. His desire to complete the mission outweighed all other options. Target acquisition still stood at ninety-nine percent, even with the anomaly. Before he sent his acknowledgment, Scout 001A reached out and touched his image. As he turned to leave, he drew his digits along his reflection, which elicited a high-pitched squeal from the metal.

*   *   *

Karl heard the unmistakable sound of metal scraping on metal on the far side of the shield. He cued Rowdy to backup and prepared for the coming attack. Instead, he heard something retreating into the distance on the opposite side of the barrier. He let out a sigh of relief as he wheeled Rowdy about to catch up with his men. As he made his way back to the column, the mist began to lift until only a light haze filled the forest. When he returned to the column, a cheer went up.

"Did you kill it?" asked Thom who was bringing up the rear of the line.

"No, it be still alive," replied Karl.

"We heard the ringing of steel from your direction and hoped all was well," said Thom.

"Aye, all be well. But we be needing to get to the Way posthaste."

"Aye, Marshal. It will be good to be done with this place," said Thom.

"Aye," said Franc who rode in front of Thom.

Karl nodded his agreement and sped up toward the front of the line. He answered questions and gave encouragement to each man as he made his way.

"That didn't take very long," said Jeri when Karl reached the head of the column.

"I only be scaring it away. We be not out o' the woods yet," repeated Karl.

Jeri nodded, a dour look on his face, before he added, "I thought as much."

Karl set a hard pace that pushed both men and horse to their limit. By mid-morning the fog had cleared and the Harkon seemed like any other wood. They had paused briefly at a brook to let the horses drink and to refill their skins and then set out again at Karl's grueling ground-eating pace.

Breaking from the heavy woods and onto the smooth gravel of the Way, Karl turned Rowdy east to Crossroads and urged him forward at a canter. Solis and Solar were nearing the horizon of the plains when the group finally stopped at a watering hole. Everyone was too drained to speak. The only sound was the labored breath of horses and men. Sweat and the sour smell of lathered leather permeated the air as man and beast took their fill of the fresh water. A darker hue of orange set in as the suns sank into the inky horizon.

Karl waited until everyone had replenished their water-skins and then addressed the men, "We be three days ride from Crossroads. I reckon that Captain Brent and the townsfolk be less than a day's ride to the east. We be the last line o' defense between that metal beastie and them." He looked to Jeri and continued, "I want ye and five men to ride ahead and be encouraging the good folk to hurry on their way."

"Aye, Marshal," acknowledged Jeri.

"The rest of us be holding the line and delaying this beastie as long as we be able," continued Karl as he looked at each man in turn. "I know we be losing Marcus today to that metal beast, and I be not wanting it to take anymore. Are ye with me, dragoons?"

"Aye," cheered the chorus of men.

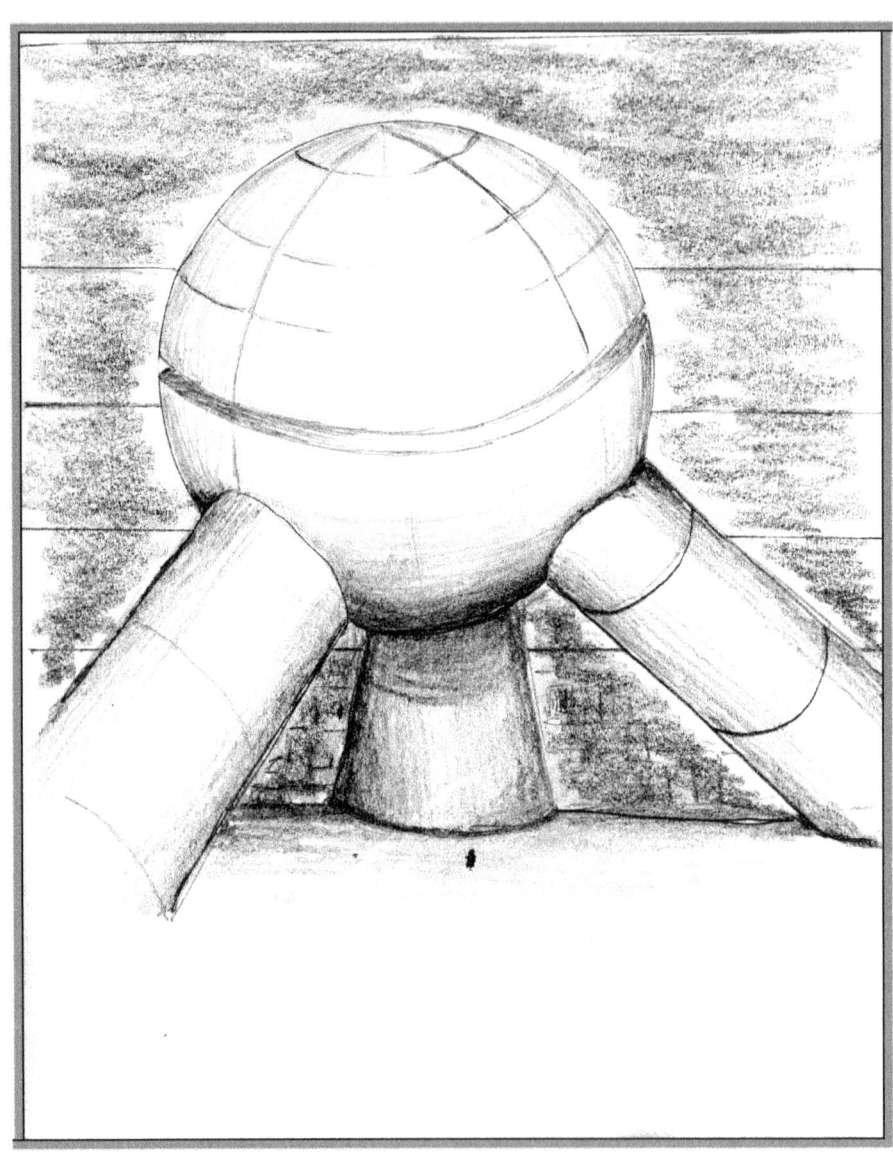

CHAPTER 17

"How big was it? It was the mountain."

-Tegain Hostler

Hours passed while Tegain sprinted up the smooth passage. In all that time there had been no sign of the metallic creatures. Only his hollow footfalls echoed back at him.

I wonder if this tunnel has an end, he thought.

I was wondering the same. It is difficult to tell time, but I do feel it has been more like a day than just a few hours.

I agree. I wonder why they tunneled so far beneath the surface, thought Tegain.

Maybe they were looking for some material that they needed.

Aye, that would make sense. I hope it isn't too much farther.

I don't think it will be, although it took us quite a while to reach Keentaa's grotto, and you've been running for some time now.

Tegain continued running up the sloped tunnel. Not long after their conversation, the terminus appeared in the distance.

I think that's it.

Yes, that is something different, agreed Lyn.

In the distance, it looked as though a shiny wall blocked the way, and the passage seemed to be made of something other than stone. Tegain slowed to a walk as he neared what appeared to be a polished metal wall. As he approached the wall, his footfalls clicked sharply on the metallic flooring of the new corridor.

"This is definitely something different," stated Tegain as he reached out to touch his reflection in the silvered wall. As soon as his mailed finger touched the surface, a line materialized in the middle of the wall. With a whoosh of air, the line split open, revealing a new passage.

Yes, very different.

A woman's voice emanated from the corridor, "Please do not be afraid. I am Gilraen. How may I assist you?"

"What is this thing?" Tegain wondered aloud.

Hmm, that is very curious. Perhaps it is an ancient relic from some long-forgotten age.

Could there be something before your time?

Are you suggesting nothing can be older than me? huffed Lyn.

Oh, by the Nine, I didn't mean that, protested Tegain.

A tingle danced down his spine.

You're laughing, aren't you?

I couldn't resist, admitted Lyn. *But in all seriousness, I honestly don't know.*

"Who are you?" asked Tegain.

"I am Gilraen," she answered.

I don't think it's an ancient relic, thought Tegain.

Yes, it may be what I suggested. Let's find out what it is.

"Where are you from, Gilraen?"

"My point of origin would have no meaning to you," replied Gilraen.

"Why are you here?"

"My prime directive is to propagate my creators' information," said Gilraen.

What does that mean? thought Tegain.

I think it means to colonize this planet.

"Why are you attacking us? Can we not live together in peace?" demanded Tegain.

Indeed, concurred Lyn.

"It has been determined that the greatest chance of mission success requires the elimination of competing organisms," Gilraen happily relayed.

Wow, she seems very pleased about wiping us out, thought Tegain.

Maybe, we can change her mind. Ask her if she has conversed with any of us before coming to her conclusion.

"Before you decided to eliminate us, did you converse with any of us?"

"No."

"Perhaps if we could talk, we could live in peace together," offered Tegain.

"Do you speak for all of your kind?"

Say yes! blurted Lyn before Tegain could speak.

"Nnn… Yes," drawled Tegain.

"Very well. Please, follow the yellow lighted pathway," said Gilraen. From the floor of the passageway, a pulsing, yellow line of light ran into the distance. "In order for us to converse in person."

What do you think? Should we proceed then?

I don't think we have much of a choice. If she is the leader of the metallic creatures, then we must find her to stop them. Be on guard though; I do not have a good feeling.

Neither do I, thought Tegain. *Very well, onward into the unknown.*

So dramatic, chuckled Lyn.

"I try my best," said Tegain, a small smile turning up the corners of his mouth.

*   *   *

Before the Dread Lord could reach the entrance at the rear of the crystal grotto, he was crushed by a wave of pain.

What is taking so long? demanded the mental voice of Hael.

The Dread Lord knew better than to give an excuse. He immediately mentally relayed images of his encounters with the false commander and replied, *I am close, my master.*

I see, responded Atos. *It appears you lack the proper motivation.*

Fiery pain consumed every fiber of the Dread Lord's being, which sent the giant staggering to his knees. Where he impacted the ground, the pain intensified a hundredfold, causing him to pitch forward onto his hands. His metal-clad palms hitting the floor felt as if he had placed them on a white-hot metal blade, only the flesh and nerves did not burn away. Regaining his feet as quickly as he could to lessen the torment, he remained stock still.

Fail me again, and you shall burn for the rest of your pathetic existence, conveyed Hael.

Yes, my master, responded the obsidian knight through the telepathic connection.

His agony ceased, and he could finally breathe. Something now dampened his cheeks. Metal clicked on metal as he touched his armored helm. A dim memory of crying when he was a child played across his mind. He clenched his plated hand and slammed it into the wall of the passageway. Stone blasted out from the blow and was instantly pulverized to dust. Metal surrounding his fist had bent and buckled, leaving the bones in his hand and forearm shattered. His ruined appendage hurt, but it was barely a fraction of what he had endured from the master. Failing the master was not an option, he knew, as he sprinted up the tunnel.

*   *   *

He followed the yellow-lit path for an immeasurable distance. After numerous twists and turns, Tegain had lost his bearings.

I have no idea where we are, he thought.

Neither do I. This is a labyrinth beyond anything I have experienced before.

I've lost count of how many turns we've made.

Ten right turns and five left turns, but there were countless passages between those.

By the Nine, cursed Tegain. *We'll never find our way out of here.*

I feel this is the intent of whoever is guiding us. However, I feel we may have crossed over our previous path several times, so we may not be as lost as we presume. I suspect that if we kept to a direct path, we would eventually find a way out.

Aye, I hope you're right. We may need to do just that.

In the distance, Tegain could see the pulsating yellow line terminating in the middle of the passageway. As he reached the end of the line, a pair of doors to his right split and disappeared into the walls to reveal a small circular room.

"Please enter," coaxed Gilraen.

"What is in there?"

"This is a lift. It will convey you to another area of my vessel," explained the feminine voice.

"All right," said Tegain dubiously. As he stepped into the room, the doors immediately whooshed shut, and the pit of his stomach wrenched as a humming sound pulsed in his ears.

Feels like I'm falling, thought Tegain.

We very well could be falling. Hold on.

Several seconds passed before he felt his gut sink along with the feeling of becoming heavier. Doors whooshed open, and the humming ceased, leaving him to wonder what had happened.

"Please exit, and follow the yellow-lit path," directed Gilraen.

Exiting the little room, Tegain found himself in a corridor that looked identical to the last one.

I hope we're actually going somewhere, he thought. *Everything looks exactly the same to me.*

I really don't have a good feeling about this.

"Please follow the yellow-lit pathway," repeated Gilraen.

Tegain remained stationary as he peered along the corridor. Magnifying his vision revealed nothing. He shared Lyn's uneasy feeling. Everything about this place seemed cold, metal, and devoid of life.

"Why can't you come to me?" he asked.

"When you see me, you will understand why I cannot come to you. Please follow the lighted path."

"By the Nine, I do not like this," said Tegain under his breath as he started out again.

I don't like it one bit either. However, it seems we do not have much of a choice.

"Aye, we've gone too far to turn back now," he said as he set out down the long corridor.

Following the highlighted pathway through several more twists and turns, they finally arrived at a towering set of double doors. With a whoosh, they split open to reveal a dark, cavernous space beyond.

"Please, enter," beckoned Gilraen.

"What is this place?" asked Tegain, studying the darkened area beyond the doors.

"This is called main engineering. I am certain it means nothing to you," informed Gilraen.

"Hmm, main engineering. Nope, I've never heard of such a place."

"This is where all the energy to sustain me through the eons is created. I am powered by a limitless quantum reactor."

"Quantum reactor? Now, I am totally lost," admitted Tegain.

As am I.

"Please, enter."

She really wants us to go in there, worried Lyn. *All the more reason not to.*

I couldn't agree more, thought Tegain. *What can we do?*

Refuse to enter and see what she does.

Dropping to one knee, Tegain leaned heavily against the door frame and asked, "Could you please come to the door? I'm too tired to go on."

"I am sorry. I cannot comply with your request," announced Gilraen. "It is just beyond the doorway. Take the time you need to recover and then proceed."

By the Nine, that didn't work, thought Tegain. *What can we do? I am at a loss. We need to stop her, but we don't know where she is or what she looks like.*

I have a strong suspicion that she knows what we intend, and she intends to destroy us.

That I do not doubt, relayed Tegain. *But that still leaves us with no clear path.*

The path is clear. However, it is fraught with unknown danger. We must prepare ourselves as best we can, then forge forward. It is either that or turn back from whence we came and perish in some other fashion.

"Well, since you put it that way," breathed Tegain. "Let us be done with this." He rose to his feet and placed Lyn upon his back. With a click that echoed in the expanse beyond, Lyn locked into place.

"Are you ready to continue?"

"I am ready to proceed, Gilraen," replied Tegain. Inhaling deeply, he took a confident step forward.

As his foot touched the metal grate in the darkened room, lights blinked on high up in the ceiling to silhouette a huge maze of metal tubes connected to a gigantic sphere.

"Welcome to Main Engineering," stated Gilraen. "Please, proceed forward."

"Is that the quantum reactor?" he said, pointing to the titanic sphere in the distance.

"Yes, it is. I am located just on the other side."

Hmm, that doesn't sound suspicious at all.

"Indeed," mumbled Tegain.

"Yes, indeed. I am."

Tegain's metallic footfalls echoed ominously throughout the dimly-lit space. Drawing closer to the monolithic globe, he had to crane his neck upward to view the smooth solid surface. Three enormous metal columns angled up to support the sphere at its base. He tried to peer beyond it, only to find a myriad of metal pipes and rope-like features. As he passed beneath the giant globe, he could hear a low hum emanating from above him. Each step brought a feeling of foreboding ever closer.

*   *   *

After several more hours spent racing up the corridor, the Dread Lord finally felt himself drawing closer to the false commander. In the distance, the passageway terminated at what appeared to be a polished metallic door. Stopping before the obstruction, he unlimbered his two-handed axe.

"Greetings. How may I assist you?" said Gilraen.

Unable to speak, the Dread Lord paused while he adjusted his grip upon the haft of his vorpal weapon.

"Are you looking for the one who calls himself Tegain?" asked Gilraen.

The goliath gave an almost imperceptible nod but otherwise remained perfectly still.

"Can you speak?"

Shrugging, the giant readied his great-axe in preparation to swing.

"Please, hold."

Cocking his black helm to the side, his red-glowing eyes pulsing, the Dread Lord waited in silence.

"Do you seek the other like you?"

The Dread Lord's eye slits flared with the mention of the false commander. He brought his two-handed axe down from his shoulder to hold the weapon before him. With a distinct nod, the giant obsidian knight confirmed Gilraen's inquiry.

"Very well."

With a whoosh of air, the mirrored metal surface slid open to reveal a long unlit corridor beyond. Recessed lights flicked on to illuminate the passageway before him.

"Please follow the lighted path," directed the soft female voice.

Tilting his head to the other side, the Dread Lord shouldered his great-axe and began cautiously traversing the foreign space. With each passing moment, his pace accelerated until he was sprinting through the cold metallic passageways.

*   *   *

Standing beneath the gargantuan sphere, Tegain felt small.

"This thing is massive."

That would be an understatement.

"It looks bigger than an entire city all put together," whispered Tegain.

A deep throbbing hum permeated the space below the sphere. He felt the vibrations in his bones. He strained his head to peer at the titanic construction above him. Examining the reactor's surface, he saw it curved outward toward the horizon. The steady thrum of machinery beat like a heart.

"I feel outmatched," whispered Tegain.

Outmatched! Against what? No creation within the material world is beyond your ability to master.

"Perhaps for you, but I'm no cynosure."

You are well on your way, my love. Together, we can face any foe.

From somewhere behind him, the swish of a distant door cut through the droning hum. Looking back to where he entered the room, Tegain saw the form of the obsidian knight blocking the entire portal.

"By the Nine," breathed Tegain. "I thought we had seen the end of him."

I as well. He is a most resilient opponent.

"He is that indeed."

Unlimbering his giant battle axe, the Dread Lord charged toward Tegain. His pounding footfalls announced impending doom. Tegain spread his feet wide, brought Lyn up into a two-handed hold next to his shoulder, and readied for the coming onslaught.

How did he find us? wondered Tegain, as the giant barreled onward.

I have a pretty good idea. I think our host's nefarious plan is finally revealing itself. I just wish I could see into her mind, but every time I try, there's nothing there. I thought we would be close enough by now.

"Well, first, let's finish this once and for all."

Indeed, she agreed as Tegain allowed her to assume control of his body.

In an instant, the dark goliath was upon them. Blade and axe blurred as they clashed beneath the quantum reactor. Time slowed for Tegain as he watched the battle through eyes he no longer controlled. Lyn's ability in combat had been acquired from centuries of battles, and her skill with the blade was unmatched. However, the necessity of preventing the edge of the weapons from touching severely limited defensive techniques.

The Dread Lord seemed to be avoiding the same. Each parry, riposte, and dirty trick ever conceived was countered. Ages seemed to pass until their strikes slowed and finally stopped. Each combatant paused, holding their weapons at the ready, waiting for the other to make a mistake. Time stood still.

From out of the silence, a piercing hum emitted from the quantum reactor. Tegain felt himself become weightless as the pulsing sound increased in tempo.

"What's happening?" he wondered aloud.

Gilraen. This… This thing above us is doing something.

"What can we do?"

Give me a moment.

Within seconds, the Dread Lord and Tegain were drawn up and helplessly pinned flat against the belly of the giant sphere. Tegain strained against the pull of the reactor's surface with all his might but to no avail.

"I am stuck," cried Tegain.

She has used some kind of cyne upon us.

"If she can cyne, why didn't she just kill us?"

I think she wants us alive.

"Well, that can't be good."

Indeed. Let's see if we cannot free ourselves from this thing.

Lyn's sweeping curves ignited into a crackling white-hot fire of pure energy. *Hold on! This is really going to hurt.*

"Hold on to what?" wondered Tegain.

Well, you know what I mean.

A thunderous discharge boomed from the blade. The entire sphere felt as if it had been lifted and dropped back down. Tegain strained under the intense pressure emitted from Lyn. It took every ounce of strength to keep from passing out. Thunder rumbled throughout the titanic room for several seconds after the blast.

"Please, stop! If my core is breached, the results will be disastrous," warned Gilraen.

That is exactly my intent. A rapid staccato of blasts hammered from the vorpal blade until Tegain could feel the force holding him to the sphere begin to weaken.

"I think it's working," cried Tegain through gritted teeth.

"Condition critical! Quantum core field system failure!" intoned a distant male voice.

Without warning, Tegain and the obsidian giant were released from the shell of the quantum reactor. Both fell heavily to the metal decking below as the entire ship shuddered with cataclysmic reverberations. Tegain slowly pushed himself up onto all fours.

"Condition critical! Reactor core breach." continued the monotonous male voice as a blaring undulating tone emanated from all directions.

"I think we should leave," said Tegain.

Indeed.

"Which way?"

Good question.

Before he could reach his feet, Tegain's breath was blasted from his lungs. He found himself hurtling through the air. Before he could gain his bearings, a crushing blow knocked him to the hard metal floor. Lying on his back, ears ringing, he tried desperately to gain his breath. As his sight and sound slowly returned, an inky shape blotted out his view.

Through his dazed senses, he could hear Lyn screaming in his mind.

Nooooooo!

Pain erupting from his arm cut off Lyn's cry. Grasping his right arm with his left hand, he recoiled reflexively into a ball. The oscillating klaxon wailed in time with his pain. Looking down at his throbbing arm, Tegain could see that his arm had been severed just below the elbow. He knew he should get up and get moving, but the shock of losing his arm kept him frozen in place.

"Lyn!" he cried out.

Silence.

"Lyn!" he screamed.

Tegain looked frantically around him. The giant sphere of the quantum reactor was beginning to crumple in upon itself. Lights flickered, and small explosions danced throughout the entire space, while the siren wailed its throbbing warning. There on the ground next to him lay his severed limb devoid of a sword. His shock from the loss of Lyn outweighed the loss of his hand. He needed to act. He needed her. She needed him.

His haze lifted, and he lurched to his feet. Cradling his damaged arm, he sprinted for the door through which he had entered. Explosions rocked the deck, knocking him into the walls of the narrow hallway. He kept to a straight path until it ended in an intersecting passageway. He chose the right corridor. It soon ended, and he then went left. He continued right and then left, snaking his way in the same direction for several more hallways until one ended in what appeared to be a doorway.

Deep within the humongous spaceship, the magnetic shielding containing the quantum reaction catastrophically failed. In an instant, the titanic globe smashed inward upon itself to the size of a pea. It was though the engine room had taken in a deep breath and held it for a brief moment. Heat, light, and sound detonated from the pea like a miniature Big Bang. Expanding outward in all directions, the force of the blast disintegrated the craft and most of the mountain it had been resting on.

Kharaxsis wheeled high above the explosion before speeding off to the west with a dark rider holding a shining sword perched upon his back.

*　　　*　　　*

After a tremendous explosion somewhere farther south in the endless peaks, Vyckie was now in danger of being buried by a series of avalanches that thundered down from every direction. To keep from being entombed by the torrent, she turned to face the coming onslaught. With her six powerful legs, she churned through the blast of snow and up the slope. As she kept her head down, her legs beating a steady staccato, the rush of snow split before her as if passing around a boulder in a stream. When the tide of snow had finally subsided, she could sense that Tegain was in great pain.

Vyckie could feel him just beyond the next range of mountains to her south. Doubling her effort, she shot up the sheer cliffs and barreled down barren slopes at a blurring pace. Hours later, she breached a saddle between two towering peaks and took pause at the scene of destruction that lay before her. What used to be a mountain was now a pool of molten slag in the floor of a large valley. She knew Tegain was down in the rapidly cooling magma.

Reaching the floor of the glowing basin, Vyckie felt him farther out in the pool of molten rock. However, there was no conceivable path to reach him. She waited. Two unbearable days passed before the cooling stone could support her weight enough to reach the area above Tegain. Driving her huge hooves down onto the brittle surface, Vyckie slowly began to chip away the obsidian rock. By the time she reached him, the feathering around her hooves had long been burnt away, and open wounds had been charred black from the heat.

Vyckie carefully chiseled away the amorphous, cooling stone encasing Tegain until she could pull him free from his tomb. She knew he lived, but still he did not move. His armor had kept him alive. She could see that his right arm was gone from just below the elbow, but the heat from the magma had cauterized the horrific wound. Nuzzling him with her soft velvet muzzle, she gently rocked his head to wake him.

*　　　*　　　*

Tegain dreamt again of the lake of fire that kept him from his beautiful Shae and Gwyn. However, this time, he heard no pleas or cries for help. He only burned. It seemed that ages had passed before a cool breeze blew upon his face. He swayed back and forth from the breeze. Eventually, a low rumble vibrated his being and the sound of thunder echoed in his ears. He was alive. Something was rocking his head and stomping the ground next to him.

"Vyckie?" Tegain groaned softly.

A high-pitched whinny accompanied another pounding of the rock near his ear.

"She's gone."

His head rocked back with the cool brush of Vyckie's tongue. She nickered softly as if to say she knew.

"We have to find her," groaned Tegain.

Vyckie responded with a lower rumble punctuated by a powerful stomp. She lowered herself down next to him. Coaxing him to take hold of her mane, she eventually urged Tegain to pull himself onto her broad back. She carefully raised herself back to her six stout legs. Setting out at a slow walk, Vyckie headed east, back to Tulane.

"No," breathed Tegain from Vyckie's back. "We must go west."

Vyckie shook her head so hard that Tegain had to hold on tightly to keep from falling off.

"Please."

Vyckie stopped, and a soft low nicker pulsated through Tegain's body.

"Yes."

Vyckie struck the fragile earth with a powerful strike that sent tiny shards of black glass in all directions.

"I'll be okay. I have you."

Vyckie huffed a blast of air that rattled her frame, and slowly turned around. Tegain fell limp against Vyckie's mighty flanks as she carefully picked her way to the west through the formidable Hittons.

*   *   *

Scout 001A had heeded the call to return to the mother ship. Gilraen was under direct attack, and all units were required to return as soon as possible. His damaged limb severely limited his ability to traverse the terrain. Perhaps, he could have it repaired when he reached home base. However, after two hours, twenty minutes, and thirty-seven seconds, Scout 001A ceased to exist. Gilraen had wiped its memory core and begun downloading her AI algorithms. Within moments, she had fully transferred her consciousness into the one of the three remaining operative left on the planet.

Gilraen had suffered a great setback. Left with this single unit, she was severely limited in her ability to complete her prime directive. However, her self-learning routines were quickly sorting through trillions of branches of outcomes to improve her chances of a positive outcome. She must propagate the information of the Seeders. This would be done.

ABOUT THE AUTHOR

Aric Carter grew up in a small town in Oklahoma. Growing up, he enjoyed playing D&D, video games, and reading science fiction fantasy books. His joy of reading followed him through his eight years of service in the US Navy. Afterward, he began writing his first book which took over nine years to complete. This his second book is the sequel to Saga of Lyn: The Reawakening.

www.ingramcontent.com/pod-product-compliance
Lightning Source LLC
Chambersburg PA
CBHW070917130626
46555CB00001B/173